"You object to my gifts?" Jason drawled

"Yes, sir," Katie snapped.

"Why?" The dark wings of his brows lifted thoughtfully.

"Gifts have strings," she insisted with a proud toss of her head. "Strings on them. You'll make a place for yourself in my boys' hearts and then you'll walk away. They have enough holes in their hearts already. They don't need any more."

"And you, Kathleen," Jason probed gently. "You give so freely, but you're afraid to take. Is that what you're afraid of, that someone will put strings on you and tie you down and then walk away?"

Her chin assumed its familiar upward thrust, daring him to challenge her. "I take care of me and mine," she said. "We don't need anybody else."

WELCOME
TO THE WONDERFUL WORLD
OF *Harlequin Romances*

Interesting, informative and entertaining,
each Harlequin Romance portrays an appealing
and original love story. With a varied array
of settings, we may lure you on an African safari,
to a quaint Welsh village, or an exotic Riviera
location—anywhere and everywhere that adventurous
men and women fall in love.

As publishers of Harlequin Romances, we're
extremely proud of our books. Since 1949,
Harlequin Enterprises has built its publishing
reputation on the solid base of quality and
originality. Our stories are the most popular
paperback romances sold in North America; every
month, six new titles are released and sold at
nearly every book-selling store in Canada and the
United States.

For a list of all titles currently available,
send your name and address to:

HARLEQUIN READER SERVICE,
(In the U.S.) P.O. Box 52040, Phoenix, AZ 85072-2040
(In Canada) P.O. Box 2800, Postal Station A
5170 Yonge Street, Willowdale, Ont.   M2N 6J3

We sincerely hope you enjoy reading
this Harlequin Romance.

Yours truly,

THE PUBLISHERS
Harlequin Romances

To Tame
a Proud Lady

Mary Fowlkes

Harlequin Books

TORONTO • NEW YORK • LONDON
AMSTERDAM • PARIS • SYDNEY • HAMBURG
STOCKHOLM • ATHENS • TOKYO • MILAN

Original hardcover edition published in 1984
by Mills & Boon Limited

ISBN 0-373-02677-3

Harlequin Romance first edition March 1985

Printed in U.S.A.

CHAPTER ONE

HOT, tired, hungry and more than a little irritated, Jason Reese braked his car to a halt and switched off the engine. From the rambling directions he had received at a gas station in Camdenton, ending with the ominous promise that he 'couldn't miss it no-how', this was the drive leading to the Staunton farm. The obstacle course he was glaring at might, with a great deal of imagination, be called a road. A better description for the narrow dirt track desperately in need of grading and crushed rock would be battlefield. It was liberally peppered with bomb-sized craters still holding the remnants of a recent rain. He'd be lucky to not break an axle.

Jason swore under his breath. Why had be punished himself with an eight-hour drive south? Why hadn't he just flown in and rented a jeep, or better still a tank? 'Stupidity,' he muttered, reaching for the suit coat and tie which had been discarded hours earlier. Hurling them back at the unoccupied passenger seat, he wiped his sweaty forehead with the back of his arm. It was too damned hot and he didn't have to impress the Staunton woman; she had to impress him, and she'd better be damned impressing!

How he'd ever let his aunt talk him into leaving his daughter with a woman he knew very little about and hadn't even seen was incomprehensible. But then Sister Claire Hannon had always had a way of making the implausible seem logical. And she had been right about sending Alicia to Holy Family School. In the single semester his daughter had been enrolled he had seen the change. The relief Alicia, a precocious seven, felt in having some kind of an ordered life had made being a part-time parent almost bearable. When Sister Claire had rattled off her list of benefits that could be gained by Alicia spending the summer in Missouri, in the Ozarks, on a farm, with children she knew and liked, with Kathleen Staunton it had sounded heaven-sent.

Later, no longer under the influence of Sister Claire's golden tongue, Jason had recognised her plan for the absurd scheme it was. The Staunton woman's fee, which was high enough, hadn't been objectionable. Even her demand to be paid by the month in advance had been understandable. It was her refusal for an interview, her refusal to even meet with him, that had roused his suspicions. Her decree that two months was the minimum time needed for Alicia to 'settle in' without the disturbing influence of her father had been the final absurdity.

Two months? Jason had given her two weeks, two weeks more than he'd been comfortable with. A maniac could do a lot of damage in two weeks, and just because she had three boys of her own it didn't mean she understood the pain of a motherless little girl. Mrs Staunton was going to answer questions now, not in seven weeks. She and her household were going to be very thoroughly examined, and if she or it were in anyway less than Sister Claire had promised, Alicia was going home with him, today.

The sole of Katie Staunton's left foot began to itch—an omen of travel in the near future. She would have preferred to have her left palm itch, a sure sign of money coming. Since she couldn't command itches and where they might locate themselves and didn't really believe in all those old mountain superstitions, she contented herself with rubbing the bare sole of her left foot against her right ankle and continued constructing sandwiches for their belated lunch.

'T.G.I.F.,' she murmured. 'Thank God it's Friday!' And what a Friday! First they had rediscovered the old playhouse furniture in the attic and lugged all that out to the playhouse and then found the dancing floor as well. Katie knew there must be a more official-sounding title for the stone-paved square that connected the back of the big house to the old wash-house turned playhouse on the north-west corner and the empty south-west corner where the summer kitchen had once stood. There must be a better name, but she didn't know what it might be. The Stauntons had always called it the dancing floor, so the dancing floor it was. The crowning moment had come when Chance, the oldest of the boys, had found the paving stone on which their grandparents had carved their initials and marriage date. It was another bit of proof that she was right; they belonged here.

Scratching her foot unleashed a dozen other itches. Wriggling her sweaty shoulder blades, Katie realised that the little ones weren't the only ones in need of a bath; she was as dirty as they were. Ripping up the grass that had crept over the dancing floor and hidden it away for forty years was hot, dirty work; and she had been in the thick of it.

She glanced out the window at the circle of five children sprawled on the tiny bit of dancing floor they had been able to uncover. She didn't need to hear their voices to know that they were discussing the best techniques for prying back the stubborn grass. Poppet, Alicia Reese, the latest addition to Katie's brood, was occupying her favourite seat, Chance's shoulder. Bo and Rocky, the middle boys, were doing a team demonstration. Jeeter, the youngest of the boys, was supplying the commentary.

Katie's generous mouth curved into a self-satisfied smile. She'd told them that they looked as if they'd been out rooting with the pigs, and even from this distance

the proof of her accusation was visible. They were
filthy. Sweat had caked dust and bits of dead grass to
their skin and there wasn't a clean head in the bunch.
She had threatened to hose them down before letting
them in the house, but now she had a better idea. They
would take their sandwiches down to the creek and
have a picnic and a swim.

Tilting her head and biting her underlip, Katie
concentrated all her energy on hearing. She recognised
the sound of a car inching its way along the lane.
Muttering words that were half prayer and half curse,
she begged that it not be the social worker, Miss Hawk,
coming for a surprise snoop. That woman was the bane
of Katie's life and in Katie's opinion for ever sticking
her long nose where it didn't belong.

'Well,' she decided with a toss of her head, 'that
woman isn't darkening this day.' She'd meet her at the
front door and send her on her way.

She didn't recognise the low-slung sports car
cautiously threading a zig-zag path along the chuck-
hole-riddled lane. It bore an out-of-state licence plate,
which most likely meant a tourist determined to find a
hillbilly loaded with antiques and too ignorant to know
their worth or a tourist on the wrong road and too
stubborn to admit it. An aggravation either way.

She stretched her hospitality to the limit and stepped
out on the front porch.

Jason flinched at what he saw. Sister Claire had told
him that the Staunton family had been in Camden
County, Missouri, for more than a hundred and fifty
years, and from the looks of things that was about the
last time anything had been built or repaired. The old
stone house and its companion outbuildings seemed to
be huddling under their patched roofs, ashamed of their
peeling paint trim. Some effort had been expended on
the surrounding lawn and old-fashioned flower beds,
but the orchard on the north side of the house had been

left to fend for itself and wasn't succeeding. An air of none too genteel poverty hung over the place, adding to Jason's already unfavourable mood.

His innate sense of fairness reminded him that old houses, even those built of stone, were in constant need of repair and that repairs were expensive and most required a man. He knew Kathleen Staunton was a woman alone struggling to raise three boys. She was probably, also, uneducated, unskilled and considered herself lucky to keep food on the table and clothes on their backs. He could understand his aunt's motive. Nuns were supposed to be charitable, but he was under no such obligation. He was a father. If things weren't much better than they looked at first glance, he was not only going to collect Alicia immediately, he was going to pay his aunt a rather warm visit before they returned to Chicago.

'Can I help you?' Katie called to the tall, broad-shouldered man who had at last deserted his car and was approaching the porch with the long, easy stride of an outdoorsman.

'Is this the Staunton farm?' Jason made a quick appraisal of the girl looking down at him from the porch and found what he saw was worthy of approval.

Tall and leggy, with curves in all the right places, she had skin the colour of wild honey. And there was so much of it showing. She was wearing a pair of low riding Levis, the legs cut off and rolled up, and a blouse that had been tied midriff and was held together by only one button. He wondered if that warm gold was her natural skin tone or if it was a tan, and if it was a tan, where did it stop. He felt a growing warmth in his loins. A man could bury his head in those breasts and sleep like a baby, if and when he got around to sleeping. And that face—there was nothing wrong with that face with its soft kissable mouth smiling provocatively at him. Even the dirty smudge on her cheek was enticing.

He noticed high, wide cheekbones and wondered if they
and the golden tint of her skin didn't come from an
Indian ancestor—a thought quickly discarded as
unlikely since she had emerald green eyes that were at
once shy and sparkling with some secret joy and honey-
gold hair shimmering with coppery fire.

Tilting her head and watching him out of the corner
of her eye, Katie considered the question and the
questioner. He was one prime example of what the male
of the species should be. Tall, several inches over her
own five foot ten, with broad shoulders tapering to
narrow masculine hips and strong thighs. There was an
aura of pride and strength surrounding him that set her
pulses racing. He walked tall, proud, his head high,
ready to meet any challenge. And when he stood he
stood with his feet firmly planted. He wouldn't run
easy. What he claimed he would keep.

'That is what the mailbox says.' She softened the bite of
her answer with a slow smile. It was a pleasure to be
noticed and frankly admired by a man, especially a man
as easy to look at as this one. There was strength and
determination in his rough-hewn face and a hint of
ruthlessness in the chiselled firmness of his mouth that
belonged to an earlier century when men carved
kingdoms out of the wilderness. Shadows hid the colour
of his deep-set eyes and accentuated the deeply etched
lines of his sun bronzed face while the sun added a
burnished warmth to his hair, the colour of hand-rubbed
walnut. His leanly muscled body should have been free of
the artificial fetters civilisation imposed, even clothes
fitting as well as his did. He was a freedom-loving, lusty
mountain man. He needed an axe over his shoulder, his
chest bared to the caress of the sun or a woman.

'Yes, it does.' A smile softened the harsh contours of
Jason's face and touched the corners of his deep-set
eyes. There was even honey in her voice, the slow,
musical drawl of the hills.

His aunt had mentioned three boys; ages fifteen, thirteen and nine. How had she ever managed to forget this girl? Reluctantly, he pulled his mind back to the business of Mrs Staunton.

'I'd like to speak to Mrs Kathleen Staunton.'

Katie's smile deepened and tongues of fire leapt through her veins. She had reason to linger under his frankly sensual spell. 'I'm Katie Staunton, and it's Miss Kathleen Staunton.'

'You're Kathleen Staunton?' Jason stared at the girl in disbelief, his shadowed eyes narrowing in shock. He knew they started young down here, but if she was the mother of a fifteen-year-old boy she had to have started having children when she was in kindergarten!

'Yes, sir,' Katie stammered, lowering her eyes, withdrawing into the wary shyness of a mountain-bred child. What had she done to merit such sudden, chilling fury?

A grimy little figure shrieking, 'Daddy! Daddy!' hurtled past Katie and threw herself at Jason.

Katie's mouth opened, but words would not come. She was suddenly, terribly aware of the stranger's identity. She had been standing on the front porch shamelessly flirting with Alicia Reese's daddy.

She had given a lot of thought to that money-grubbing, low-down, weasel-hearted, Yankee peddler Jason Reese in the last two months. Ever since Sister Claire, principal of the school she had graduated from and her brothers still attended, had introduced her to Alicia and relayed his proposal, Katie had been wanting to kick him up one side of a mountain and down the other. How any man could just dump his child on a stranger's doorstep like so much dirty laundry went beyond Katie's understanding. Not only had he been too busy to personally meet with her while school was still in session and Alicia, re-christened Poppet, was visiting on alternating weekends, but he hadn't been able to tear himself away from his precious computers since school ended two weeks ago. Not that it had been put just that way. His message, relayed through Sister Claire, had had a much loftier ring. He felt that Alicia shouldn't be subjected to the pull of two families. He felt that two months of totally experiencing the Stauntons was the minimum time necessary for the child to acclimatise. His own damning words from his own mouth, once removed. How Katie had longed to meet him and give him the sharp edge of her tongue! Now she couldn't even make her mouth work.

But then in all those confrontations Katie had rehearsed in her mind Jason Reese had been older, short and paunchy, pale from the lack of sunlight, mean-looking with a sly weasel face and often possessing a forked tail and cloven hooves. Never had she considered the possibility that he might be an excitingly virile man.

Jason scooped Alicia up in his arms and hugged her tightly. God, how he'd missed her! Since the death of his wife, Ann, four years ago, Alicia was the only thing that made life worth living. Gently, he brushed a dead leaf from her tangled blonde hair.

His feelings as a man and a father collided. This wasn't the middle-aged widow he had envisaged, pleasantly plump and smelling of freshly-baked cookies. How dared she, this Kathleen Staunton, be so young and stand there looking so ripe and ready for love and at the same time innocent of a man's touch? Her, with three sons and so obviously proud of not being married that she'd not only told him but seemed pleased about it. And his Alicia, his princess—what had she done to her? She was filthy, her fragile body hidden under layers of sweat and dirt, and she was dressed up in some grubby costume a hobo wouldn't want.

His clashing emotions generated anger. What had the girl done with the money he'd sent? Obviously she hadn't spent it on soap and water or anything else for Alicia.

'Are you suffering a shortage of soap and water, Miss Staunton?'

His words were sharp, cold knives slicing at her heart. The barely caged fury and icy contempt in those few words immobilised Katie, body and mind. She could do nothing more than hang her head and wait for the explosion that didn't come. Cautiously she raised her eyes to his chest and saw what he saw—Poppet, a very dirty Poppet.

'No, sir,' she whispered.

'A clothing famine, perhaps,' Jason growled.

'No, sir.' She wanted to explain about the cut-off blue jeans and faded chambray shirt the child was wearing, Jeeter's hand-me-downs and Poppet's pride and joy. They had been clean just that morning and so had Poppet. Katie wanted to explain, but her tongue stuck to the roof of her mouth.

A low, rumbling grumble echoed through the unnatural silence, Poppet's empty belly demanding its share of their three-hour-overdue lunch. Gathering together the tattered shreds of her pride, Katie raised her chin to a haughty angle and stared past Jason. She could explain everything to his satisfaction if given a chance, and she wouldn't say one word about his shameful neglect.

'We were about to eat lunch. Would you care to join us, sir?'

The dark wings of Jason's brows gathered in disbelief. His daughter bore a striking resemblance to a rag picker, and this woman thought she was a queen issuing invitations to a royal banquet!

'I believe my daughter possesses a pair of shoes?'

'Shoes?' Katie echoed, her heart plummeting. She could explain how one little girl could get so dirty in a matter of hours. She could explain why blue jeans were

better for tree climbing and treasure hunting than the
frilly dresses that constituted Poppet's wardrobe. But
never in a million years could she explain how Alicia
Reese had become shoeless, not to a man who didn't
want to listen.

Only the night before had she noticed the red marks
the too small dress sandals, worn only a few hours, had
rubbed on Poppet's feet. Katie had been so upset with
herself for not noticing before, she'd gathered up every
pair of outgrown shoes in the house and burned them
all. She'd meant to buy new shoes this morning. She'd
meant to, but until now the rush of a dozen other things
had pushed the need for shoes completely from her
mind.

'Yes, Miss Staunton,' Jason's anger chilled look
swept from her face to her feet, as bare and dusty as
Poppet's, 'shoes—some people wear them on their feet.'

Her eyes fastened on her own bare feet, Katie shook
her head and whispered a slow, miserable, 'No, sir.'
Alicia Reese had no shoes. They'd all been too small;
Poppet had hit a growing spurt.

'I see,' his deep voice rumbled ominously out of his
broad chest. 'You have one hour, Miss Staunton'—
again Jason laid heavy emphasis on her unmarried
state—'to have my daughter's belongings packed and
waiting. Or am I being rash to assume she has some
articles of clothing left?'

The tears stinging her eyes and swelling in her throat
choked any explanation Katie might have made. Jason
didn't wait for any explanation. He turned on his heel
and carried his struggling daughter away.

A shrill howl jerked Katie out of her misery in time
to catch Jeeter, the youngest of the boys, as he crashed
through the screen door, intent on pursuing the stranger
making off with their Poppet.

'Katie!' he wailed, his arms and legs flailing at her
restraining body.

'That's just Poppet's daddy come to take her home,' she whispered, drawing the boy close, sharing his ache.

'He can't have her!' he screamed, as much to the retreating automobile as to Katie.

'Yes, he can.' Katie buried her face in his new-penny-bright hair. 'Oh, yes, he can.'

'What do you want us to do, Katie?' Chance, the oldest of the boys at fifteen and the man of the house, spoke quietly, but his hands were clenched in fists and his jaw was set in anger.

Katie tossed her head, blinking back tears. She wasn't sure how much they'd heard, but it had been enough. The older three wouldn't vent their anger as readily as Jeeter, but it was there, smouldering in their eyes. Alicia was their Poppet and her removal demanded retaliation. Katie understood, but she could not allow it. Shoving aside her own jumbled feelings, she tackled the problem of cooling tempers. She and they needed at least the outward semblance of normalcy. Food was normal and a good place to start.

'The first thing I want you all to do is eat. Then I'm going to change into something a little more civilised than this get-up.' Attempting a wry smile, Katie unrolled the frayed edges of her faded denim shorts and undid the shirt tails she had tied up to just under her breasts while excavating the dancing floor and tried not to notice how little time Jason Reese lost in leaving or remember the thrill of anticipation that had run through her veins when he'd first looked at her.

'Now, you all just put yourselves in Mr Reese's shoes. You just think about how you'd feel if the first time you laid eyes on us this is what you saw.' She raked the quartet of boys with a look of haughty disdain. 'You all look like you've been out rooting with the pigs. That's exactly what I said, didn't I? And I'm used to seeing you dirty.'

'Yes, ma'am,' they chorused dutifully with surreptitious glances at their grubby clothes and grimy bodies. They were a disgrace to Katie's good name.

Katie nodded, her generous mouth pressed into a firm line as she examined each of the four boys with careful scrutiny designed to further cool their lust for revenge. When they were properly abashed, she hummed her agreement.

'And it isn't bad enough that we had to look like this. So did Poppet.' She paused, giving them a few moments to ponder the full meaning of that charge. They also preferred seeing Poppet in ruffles and bows. 'Now, Mr Reese is coming back in one hour, and when he does, we're all going to look a little more presentable. Then we, he and I, will sit down and discuss our little misunderstanding—and that's all it is, a little misunderstanding. You'll see, everything is going to be all right.'

'Yes, ma'am,' they mumbled in unison, more because they wanted to agree with whatever Katie said and ease the pain in her eyes than because they believed.

The four boys, under Katie's watchful eyes, wolfed the sandwiches she had prepared, washing down what changed to sawdust and cardboard in their mouths with a gallon of fresh milk that was equally tasteless.

Katie, feeling a fresh rush of tears threatening, hastily turned and rewiped and polished the kitchen counter she had just cleaned. She couldn't let them see that she had any doubts.

Four pairs of eyes met, exchanging a grim, silent vow. *He* had not only stolen their Poppet, *he* had made their Katie cry. They were going to get *him*, but good!

Chance cleared his throat and shot the others a warning glance to follow his lead. 'I think I'll go on over to the Spencers' and see if Mr Spencer needs me for haying Monday. The little ones want to go along. Maybe we'll stop for a swim on the way back.'

'Why, I——' Katie bit her lip and scrubbed the clean

counter some more. Walking to the neighbouring Spencer farm, admiring the old car Chance was buying from Bobby Ray Spencer, swimming, all that would occupy them for at least two hours. She'd heard Jetter's earnest wish to, 'bash his head in but good', and the others shushing him. Having those four safely away would allow her to concentrate entirely on winning Jason Reese over to her point of view. But if they, for even a moment, suspected she wanted them gone they'd stick like glue. A not too subtle insult aimed at their fledgling male egos was the surest way to steer them in the direction she wanted them to go.

'Checking with Mr Spencer would be more courteous than just calling. But that's a bit of a walk. You other three sure you want to tag along all that way on such a hot day?'

Chance shrugged casually. 'If Jetter gets tired I can always carry him piggyback.'

'Carry me?' Jetter spluttered, favouring his oldest brother with a genuinely murderous glare. 'I can walk the legs off you any day, boy!'

Bo and Rocky, older than Jeeter but younger than Chance, jerked their chins down in agreement with Jeeter. They'd walk the legs off him too.

Satisfied that the injured egos were puffing nicely, Katie turned to polishing the sink and missed the exchange of triumphant looks.

The boys safely gone, Katie dropped her pretence of cleaning and raced upstairs. An hour wasn't very long and twenty minutes had already been wasted. She packed Poppet's frilly wardrobe, ignoring the little twist of pain her heart felt as each garment disappeared into the belly of the suitcase. She would get Poppet back. She would make everything right. She had been foxing, outwitting 'them' for almost five years; she could do it again. 'Them' meaning anyone not a Staunton, relative or close friend but most particularly anyone who suffered the delusion of thinking that he or she could tell the Stauntons what they could or could not do.

Snorting her contempt for 'them', Katie skinned out of her clothes and stepped into the shower. She scrubbed her golden skin, which was only slightly paler where the sun had not touched, until it glowed. Mr Jason Reese objected to barefoot hillbillies, did he? Well, she'd just introduce him to Kathleen Staunton, a proud and intelligent woman capable of running a business, facing down judges and confounding social workers. She'd convince him that his eyes had lied; then they could settle their difference of opinion like two rational adults.

Katie's confidence edged upward. Poppet was a talker and a charmer. It hadn't taken her long to get the boys right where she wanted them, under her thumb. Her father would be even more susceptible to those deep blue, thickly-lashed eyes that could produce a single tear whenever Alicia wished. Right now, this very minute, Katie assured herself, Jason Reese was having his mind changed for him.

And if he didn't change his mind? Katie wouldn't allow herself to even think such a thing could happen. Poppet was theirs, she belonged in the old house as surely as any of them. She had filled a hole in their lives none of them had even known was there until she came. Katie, who could never resist a child, had felt the tug on her heart the first time she had seen Alicia Reese, so little and forlorn, in the school yard. Jeeter had already been a casual friend from a shared reading class, but now they were inseparable. Even Bo and Rocky, the budding scientists and their own closed corporation, allowed Poppet in their lab, an unprecedented happening. Chance, an easy target for anything little and cuddly, was totally enthralled. And Poppet— Poppet needed them as much as they needed her. Here she wasn't different. Nobody in this house had a mother and they all knew that there were times when a hug and no questions was what was needed. No, he couldn't take her away. They'd all lost enough already, Katie wouldn't allow it.

'Why couldn't you have come this morning?' she asked the air. Morning, the very short time after the strawberries they sold were delivered and before Poppet and Jeeter got down to the serious business of treasure hunting. Morning, that precious time when the little ones were going-to-town neat and clean. 'Or, better still, tomorrow,' Katie begged. Tomorrow, when she wouldn't be preoccupied with attic treasure and discovering the dancing floor and would remember such ordinary things as buying needed shoes.

But he hadn't come tomorrow, he'd come today, and drawn the worst possible conclusions. Since bewailing that the fates couldn't change that, Katie had to. The memory of Jason Reese, so totally male, so totally unlike what she had expected, stole into her conscious mind. Twisting the taps to off and grabbing a towel, she ignored the flutter that began in her stomach and radiated out to her fingertips and toes. So he wasn't the little man with the sly, weasel face she had expected. He still had a sly, little weasel soul, she assured herself, and that was the true measure of a man.

With practised ease, she twisted the shimmering mass of her hair into a coil on the nape of her slender neck, a style she fancied added maturity and sophistication to her face. Gnawing on her underlip, she stared at the mirror and considered the results and her knowledge of men. While no one had ever told her in so many words, she knew that all men had been created a little soft in the head. Any woman worth the name *woman* could manipulate a man. It was all in knowing how, and Katie Claire Staunton knew how. Jason Reese might not be as easy as some, she admitted reluctantly, but he could be brought around. She simply had to choose the right method. Coy and flirtatious, cool and stand-offish, intelligent or scatterbrained, she could be any of those things, anything except talkative, and men didn't want their women talkative, they wanted them to listen. Which should she be? She knew from Sister Claire that he owned an electronics company and built computer systems. Yes, she nodded her agreement to her mirror reflection, that was the key to winning him over—computer. He built them because he had a mind like one. She would present her argument in terms a computer could understand, a cold, heartless computer.

His personality firmly settled in her mind, Katie scanned her limited wardrobe. Buying clothes for herself ranked well down on her list of priorities. She shrugged away the beginnings of self-pity; possessing only two good outfits simplified choosing. Since she had come very close to wishing for something feminine and seductive, she chose the severely tailored navy blue pants suit usually reserved for lawyers and bankers.

Scrubbed and clothed in what she hoped was suitable for impressing a computer, she went to wait in her parlour, hoping that she was the spider and he the fly.

After congratulating herself on being ready ten minutes early, she discovered that sitting and waiting was even worse than rushing to be ready. She paced the living room, stopping at every mirror to make sure no trace of the barefoot hillbilly girl Jason Reese found so objectionable had eluded her.

The big living room wasn't big enough. She strolled through the dining room and kitchen, poked her head into the pantry and downstairs bathroom. She noticed a dirty handprint on the moulding by the bathroom door and regretted her decision to put off scrubbing the back hall until a rainy day. She bypassed the unused room that had once been the housekeeper's and let herself into the study by the back hall door. Finding no comfort in the leather chair and massive desk that had been her father's, she completed the circuit of the downstairs by passing through the small parlour and returning to the big living room.

'Come on!' she hissed under her breath. Waiting gave her too much time to notice how shabby everything was becoming, time to wish there were no such things as ice storms and drunken drivers, time to wish her father was there to brilliantly argue her cause and her mother to apply her special soothing charm. But drunken drivers were real and so were ice storms and the fatal accidents that resulted from such lethal combinations. Wishing wouldn't change the fact that the drunk had survived his handiwork and her parents hadn't. Wishing accomplished nothing and prayers not much more, but Katie Claire Staunton could and would. She'd handle Jason Reese just as she'd handled all the problems that had come knocking on her door, because there was nothing else to do and no one else to do it.

At last she heard the sound of a car turning in the lane. Moistening her lips with the tip of her tongue, Katie checked the mirror one last time. He's not a man, she reminded her erratic pulse, only Poppet's daddy. And there'd be no more flirting or even thinking about it.

'Mr Reese.' Katie bobbed her head at the man standing on her front porch and pushed the screen door open wide. Her traitorous heart quivered under the spell of his powerful masculinity and eyes that she could now see were the crystal blue of an autumn sky and holding the same hint of frost.

He declined her invitation with a curt shake of his dark head and noted her transformation with a ghost of a knowing smile.

Prodded by feelings she didn't want, Katie's temper soared. Resolutely she shoved aside the pleasure of becoming angry. She was going to remain cool and calm and reasonable if it killed her.

'I wanted to explain about this evening,' she stated in her best Businesswoman Kathleen voice.

'There's no need,' Jason assured her, his words as cool and sharp as a winter day.

'There is a need, for my own satisfaction if nothing else,' Katie snapped. Biting her lip, she lowered her eyes. That was no way to convince him. No tantrum or gush of tears or fluttering lashes, for that matter, would convince Jason Reese, of that she was certain. Like one of his computers he understood only facts.

'Children get dirty, it's a fact of life, but God in His wisdom made them washable. Poppet was scrubbed at frequent intervals, and fed too.' She made no mention of love, which was impossible to measure in terms a computer could understand.

'Alicia has been quite adamant in your defence, Miss Staunton. I understand that it isn't every day that a dancing floor is discovered. And as for the outgrown shoes, that was as much my fault as yours—shoes aren't outgrown in a day or even two weeks. I should have noticed.'

Katie's hopes crumbled. He wasn't supposed to accept the blame for Poppet's shoeless state so easily. Calm and rational people were only calm and rational when they had made up their minds—irrevocably. There had been a note of condescension, almost amusement, in his voice when he had mentioned the dancing floor. He was telling her that she had done her best but her best wasn't quite good enough.

She raised her eyes to a point just beyond his left shoulder, her chin angled proudly. There was no changing his mind, take Poppet he would, but he'd take a piece of her mind with him.

'She is a child, not some china doll to be set on a shelf and admired and played with when the fancy strikes you. She needs to be touched and loved—and yes, even to get dirty once in a while.'

'Her suitcases, please.' With a great deal of effort Jason kept his voice level. Alicia had been more than adamant, she had threatened a hunger strike if she was not returned to this bewitching woman-child who was now lecturing him on the care of his own child.

'The suitcases? Oh my, yes, the suitcases,' Katie raged, her chin attaining an even more haughty angle, her eyes snapping green fire. 'To hell with the child, just don't forget the damn suitcases! I'll get them—it won't take me but a minute. You just wait right here.'

She went the long way round to get the suitcases which were waiting by the bottom of the front stairs, detouring through her father's study. Stopping at her own small drop-front desk, she snatched up the uncashed cheque Jason had sent by registered mail. She'd make sure he got back more than the requested return receipt. That cheque had sent her blood boiling the minute she'd first seen it. It was a business cheque, typed and with a stub detailing, in neat little rows, exactly what it was for, forty-three days of child care, dates and all. She was going to have the great pleasure of throwing it in his face, Mr Jason Almighty Dollar Reese. And he could just stick that in one of his computers and see what happened!

Dumping the suitcases at his feet, she held out the hated cheque, her spine ramrod-stiff, her eyes flashing defiance.

When Jason recognised the paper being thrust at him as a cheque, his cheque, he waved it aside. He had no doubt that she needed it far more than he did. He was a concerned father, not a monster. His surprise that the cheque hadn't been cashed roughened his voice, 'The cheque is yours, Miss Staunton.'

'No, sir.' Stern mountain pride steadied her trembling legs and added a disdainful edge to her voice. She wasn't a shoeless hillbilly. She wasn't in need of his charity. Taking money for loving a child had gone against her sense of open-handed hospitality from the very beginning. Only Sister Claire's forceful reminders that child care was a tax-deductible expense which Jason Reese would expect and need for his taxes had allowed her to exchange money for caring. Even so, she hadn't been able to lower her pride far enough to cash that cheque. And she definitely wasn't going to take money for not keeping a child, especially not from him.

'I insist, in lieu of notice.' His voice took on the steely quality of a man not accustomed to being told no.

When Jason refused again, his strong jaw hardening against his ridiculous desire to relent and tell her that Alicia was hers if she would take him too, Katie tore the cheque in half. Her own mouth set as firmly as his, she ripped the halves in half again and then shredded the quarters.

'This is my house and I do the insisting here. I didn't take Poppet for money, I kept her for love, and you can't buy love.' She allowed the shreds of paper to filter through her fingers in a final act of defiance.

'Then you will understand when I say that I love my daughter and that I must do what I think best for her, not necessarily what she wants.' His hard, closed face softened for a moment and his glacial blue eyes mirrored regret.

'Yes, sir,' Katie whispered, ducking her head. 'I can understand that.' She bit her lower lip to control its trembling. Somehow she did understand. The computer had a heart, he loved Poppet, and it was a love strong enough to say 'no' when 'yes' was easier. She loved the boys the same way. He was wrong, but she had been too. An apology was owed and due. Tossing her head, she blinked back the threatening mist of tears.

'I think you're mistaken, Mr Reese, but that's your privilege. I do apologise for the state you found us in this evening but not for the care we gave Poppet.' She realised that was a stiff-necked excuse for an apology, but it was the best she could do. He was tearing a piece of her heart out by the roots. She fled before she totally disgraced herself by bursting into tears.

Without a word or a sign, Jason bent to pick up the suitcases. He felt an almost overwhelming urge to go out and get roaring drunk. She made him feel like a two-headed monster, which was absolutely insane. He wasn't stealing her child, simply reclaiming his own for the good of all involved.

CHAPTER TWO

'MISS STAUNTON!'

The icy rage in Jason's voice jerked Katie to her feet and out the door. He glared up at her from the bottom porch step, his hands spread against his thighs, his heaving chest straining the fine fabric of his shirt. 'Get them out here.'

'What?' Katie managed to gasp. She had no idea what he was demanding be brought to him. Poppet's clothes were all in her suitcases and the shoes were ashes—he couldn't possibly want them.

'Those hooligans you call boys have kidnapped my daughter! I have the ransom note.'

Katie leaned against the rough stones of the house, her legs threatening to desert her. She didn't doubt for a minute what he was saying. She should have realised that they were too eager to be gone. They'd done it.

'John Carter! Charles Allen! Robert Lee! Randall Lee!' Katie called, her panicked recital of their full names a warning to appear immediately or suffer dire consequences.

Jeeter and Chance strolled around the corner of the house, a picture of unhurried innocence.

'You want us, Katie?' Jeeter grinned his most angelic smile.

'Get her,' Chance ordered, shoving Jeeter in the direction of the barn. Squaring his shoulders, he faced a wrathful Jason Reese and an ashen Katie. He was the oldest of the boys and responsible for their actions. 'Katie didn't know anything about it—it was my idea. I reckon you'll be wanting this too.'

Katie's world threatened to roll into a ball and turn

upside down. She wasn't particularly mechanically inclined, but she did know what a distributer cap looked like and what it did. They hadn't only stolen his daughter, they had disabled his car as well.

She heard a muffled disturbance in the house and Rocky hiss, 'Give me that gun!'

Her face rearranged itself into a desperate grimace. 'If you'll excuse me, please, for a moment, Mr Reese.'

She slipped through the door and into the house. Bo and Rocky were in the living room wrestling over the Long Tom. It made no difference that the shotgun hadn't been fired in maybe fifty years, or that they didn't even have shells for it, or that the one pulling the trigger, if they had found shells for it, was in far more danger of being blown apart than the one aimed at. The man was right, this was no place for Poppet. It wasn't a house, it was a loony-bin.

She separated the pair, none too gently, and took the gun. 'Sit!' she hissed under her breath, jerking her thumb towards the couch. With a look that promised bloody murder and general mayhem if they so much as wiggled wrong, she propped the useless weapon in a corner.

Dusting her hands of the pair perched on the couch, she took a deep steadying breath and went back to face Jason Reese, who now had more than just cause to take Poppet as far from them as he could possibly get her.

Jeeter and Poppet had stopped halfway between the barn and the house, his arm wrapped protectively around her shoulders. Chance knelt in front of them. He brushed wisps of straw from her clothes and hair, then carefully wiped the dust from her new shoes. Jeeter smoothed a mussed curl in place, and Poppet buried her face in his chest.

Katie squeezed her eyes shut. They had done a cruel and worrysome thing to Jason Reese, but if she was nine years old and an adult was stealing her Poppet and the only other adult present had failed to prevent it, she would have schemed desperate schemes too. It was her fault. She was the responsible one; she should have known and stopped them.

Chance swept Poppet into his arms, then tossed her in the air and caught her and hugged her, their everyday greeting which never failed to produce giggles and demands for more. This time, though, Poppet hid her face in his shoulder and clung to him.

Ignoring her father, Chance gave Poppet to Katie. His face was set, he had done wrong, he would accept whatever punishment Katie deemed fitting and proper, but he wasn't about to give their Poppet to him.

Poppet wound her arms around Katie's neck. 'I'm coming back, Katie,' she whispered.

Katie set Poppet down and knelt before her. She tilted the stubborn little chin up and forced those vividly blue eyes, so like Jason's, to look only at her. They had done enough to the man already. She could not encourage any more chicanery.

'Now, you be a good Poppet for your daddy,' Katie warned, her tender heart breaking. 'You hear me, child, don't you do anything to worry him.'

Shocked by her betrayal, Poppet stared at Katie, her underlip quivering, a tear trembling in the corner of her eye. Katie was torn apart, but she knew what she had to do. She wrapped the child in one last hug before lifting her into her father's waiting arms.

There was a distance between Katie and the boys far greater than the few feet separating them. Their hearts were broken, their world shattered, and she had made them do chores and pick strawberries. In their averted eyes she had become the unfeeling money-grubber she had so often called Jason Reese in her mind.

It wasn't often that the brood included Katie among the faceless 'them' as opposed to 'us'. Being so firmly shut out of their circle hurt. But that was a hurt she had accepted when, after the deaths of their parents, she had refused the offers to take this or that boy and had stubbornly insisted that they would stay on the farm, together. She was more than their big sister, she was their legal guardian, the responsible one. Part of those responsibilities was financial. Nursing broken hearts today wouldn't make it any warmer in January when the fuel bill came—only strawberries picked and sold every day from May through September could do that.

Rubbing the back of her neck, Katie began re-counting the boxes of berries for Callahan. With no Poppet bouncing around, counting out loud, she couldn't concentrate. One, two, three, four, five, six, seven. Once more the flats and boxes of berries blurred, forcing her to begin again. Glaring at the wavering boxes of berries, she reminded herself that the only thing crying ever did was give her a headache.

At last she nodded; the count was full. They were done for the night. The three older boys dropped down on the back porch, huddling close together. Jeeter rubbed his bare toes across an uncovered stone, Poppet's dancing floor. He didn't care about any ol' dancing floor, but she did. They'd done it for Poppet. If the others were miserable, he was devastated, and not just because Poppet had rescued him from the unmanly position of being the least one, the baby of the family. She was his best friend and partner. He didn't even mind playing house with her. Head drooping, he went around the corner to mourn in private.

Moments later Jeeter tore around the corner of the house, his arms flapping, his eyes wide. 'Get your gun, Bo,' he panted, ''cause he's back!'

'Don't . . . you . . . dare!' All the hurt and humiliation she had suffered hardened Katie's voice to a low-pitched threat that halted the battle-ready quartet on the first porch step. 'You four have already stolen his child, disassembled his car and tried to shoot him. Enough,' she stamped her foot, 'is enough!'

Bo slunk down under the weight of her wrath. 'I wasn't really going to shoot him, Katie. I was just going to scare him a little.'

'Scare him a little?' Katie repeated. 'You'd all better consider yourselves real lucky if he didn't come back here with the entire State Militia behind him!'

The legal repercussions of their actions slammed down on their young shoulders and squashed any idea of further retaliation out of their minds.

'What are we going to do, Katie?'

'You all are going to ask Mr Reese to kindly step inside and sit down. Then you all are going to tell him that I'll be in directly. You all will say nothing else. You all will do nothing else. You all hear me?'

They nodded in unison, barely daring to breathe. Katie's temper at full boil was a truly awesome thing.

'Do I make myself understood, Charles Allen Staunton?'

'Yes, ma'am.' Being the next oldest and the next most responsible, Chance squared his shoulders and readied himself to take whatever was coming.

'Robert Lee Staunton?'

'Yes, ma'am.' Bo squirmed under her blazing anger. Almost one of the older ones, he should have known better.

'Randall Lee Jackson!' Katie's anger softened. Rocky was already thoroughly contrite and frightened. Plus, he was the one who had tried to disarm Bo.

'Yes, ma'am.'

'John Carter Staunton?'

'Yes, Katie. Yes, ma'am,' Jeeter gasped between breaths, nodding, his eyes darting from her to the others, to the corner around which he expected the devil himself to appear any moment.

'Get!' Katie ordered.

With the boys dispatched to act as an official greeting party, Katie rested her head against a porch post. Her stomach knotted painfully. Like the boys, she hadn't considered the possibility of the law until she spoke the words. Northerners were notorious for calling the law for any little thing, and this day's work went some past any little thing. Neither tears nor pretty excuses would move him if he'd made up his mind to go to the law. That firm mouth and those deep lines etched in his sun-bronzed face told of a man used to having his own way.

Used to having his own way with women too, Katie thought as she jerked off the faded bandana protecting her hair and shook her head until the tousled mane of sun-gold and copper tumbled freely down her back. She frowned derisively, not that she had anything to worry about that way. Not even if she was declared the lost and found Queen of Sheba and stood before him dripping ermine and diamonds would he ever see anything other than a barefoot hillbilly girl with a dirty face.

She took special care to erase any possibility of lingering garden dust and added a dab of lip-gloss for good measure. She shook her head at the idea teasing her mind. She would not change her clothes again. He'd already seen her at her worst and at what was supposed to be her best, and neither meeting had exactly been a success. A masquerade wouldn't impress him. She seldom wore shoes in the house, in summer she padded barefoot and in winter wore soft slippers. It was simple preference and had nothing to do with the place of her birth. If by some miracle Jason did not press charges and did allow Poppet to return he would make that discovery soon enough. She also enjoyed the freedom of Levis, soft and faded to the point of comfort. There was no shame in old, only in dirt. Through good times and bad no Staunton had ever crawled, and she wasn't about to start at this late date.

Head high, she strolled into the living room. 'Mr Reese,' she acknowledged his presence with a barely perceptible inclination of her proud head and made a royal procession of one to the bentwood rocker across the room from the love seat he occupied. Silent and haughty in faded denim, she sat in her rocking chair throne and waited.

Poppet, sharing the love seat with her father, wiggled until he laid a restraining hand on her leg. 'I get to stay, Katie.' She giggled and disappeared behind his intimidating presence.

Jeeter yelped and bounced out of the couch before the others could politely jerk him back. Katie shot him an icy warning on expected deportment. She forced her face to remain coolly remote, but her heart was pounding and she couldn't keep her eyes from sliding expectantly in Jason's direction.

'If we can agree on certain conditions,' Jason amended, bringing the line-up of four boys to the edge of the couch. 'I believe there was an interview that should have taken place some time ago, Miss Staunton.'

'Yes, of course, Mr Reese,' Katie agreed in a tone that matched his cool, businesslike tone. She floated across the room on a cloud of hope, her feet barely making contact with the plush carpet with its muted design of birds and flowering vines. 'If you will follow me.'

She was amazed to discover that she could speak entire, coherent sentences and even gesture him to follow her when her heart was beating a wild clog dance against her ribs and her knees were shaking in three-quarter time.

Pausing to pull the double oak doors out of their nesting place in the walls, she allowed a proud smile to touch the corners of her mouth. She had never been more grateful to the Stauntons who had come before her than she was now. In their wisdom, they had created a home that in its sturdy simplicity had stood the test of time well. He couldn't fail but be favourably impressed. The outside walls were twenty-two-inch thick native stone and as weather-tight as they had been in 1834. The highly polished oak floors framing the antique wool carpets covered solid oak subfloors and beams. From attics to cellars there wasn't a bit of dry rot or damp.

Pride tilted Katie's chin as she strolled through the smaller of the two living rooms, more properly called the ladies' parlour. It didn't take an expert to know that the furnishings were genuine and that most dated to an era before the war between the States. Jason might consider the lady of the house a barefoot hillbilly, but he would have to see that she sprang from good stock.

She slid open another pair of doors and motioned him to precede her. She chose the study as the site for their delayed interview with good reason. It was a genuine library. Two walls were lined with books, from floor to ceiling, many impressively leather-bound and gilted. The Stauntons were educated hillbillies. It also offered the greatest privacy. They could not be overheard by five pairs of flapping ears. Most important, as it was the room furthest from the living room the distance and closed doors would muffle the outbreak to the level of a controlled roar when the expected victory whoops erupted.

He did not sit down and thereby give her the psychological advantage of standing and looking down at him. Jason leaned against the corner of her father's desk, his long legs stretched out in front of him. The power of his masculinity sent a shiver skittering down her spine. He reminded her of a powerful jungle cat, lithe and tautly muscled, waiting to strike and crush its prey in its powerful grasp.

She resisted the urge to scamper for the nearest hiding place, but she knew how helpless a mouse must feel when it sticks its head out and finds the cat waiting. She moved at a sedate pace to a seat far enough from him to curb his disturbing effect on her pulse and uncomfortable enough to keep her from forgetting that she was the mouse this jungle cat was stalking.

Sitting primly erect, with her trembling hands loosely curled in her lap, Katie made use of her most effective weapon, silence. Jason also well versed in the power of silence allowed it to descend like a heavy cloud until it filled the room.

'Your father was Thomas A. Staunton? The late State Senator Staunton?'

'Yes, sir. Before that he was a county magistrate and an attorney in private practice,' Katie elaborated with a certain allowable pride.

'Your parents died following an automobile accident?' his voice dipped sympathetically.

'Yes, sir.' There was a slight hiss of pain in Katie's answer, for her parents, the boys, herself, pain quickly masked by anger. She wasn't asking for charity. She hadn't asked for help when her parents were dying and she hadn't asked after, when the hospital and doctor bills had gobbled everything. The Stauntons took care of their own and outsiders stayed out. All of them, relatives, neighbours, friends, governments, she didn't need or want any of them sticking their noses in her business or feeling sorry for her or hers.

'I'm not trying to pry, but I do need to clarify certain points, in my own mind,' Jason continued, reminding himself that he was interviewing an employee and one requiring a great deal of clarification. The report his office had relayed regarding one Staunton, Kathleen C. had raised more questions than it answered.

'I understand,' Katie murmured stiffly. A part of her mind did understand that he needed to know the background of the woman charged with the safekeeping of his daughter. None the less, someone snooping around in her life was an irritation she hadn't endured often and never willingly.

'Your "boys" are in truth your younger brothers?' Jason enquired casually, resisting the urge to force those eyes so stubbornly focused on the floor to look at him. He wanted to tell her that he wasn't Simon Legree, he didn't beat little girls, especially those who had matured so bewitchingly.

'Yes, sir.' Forgetting her manners, Katie stared at him, her bewilderment clouding her eyes to the green-gold of spring moss. 'What else would they be?'

'Yes, and how old are you? Twenty? Twenty-one?' Jason tersely demanded, ignoring her question.

'Twenty-three.' Katie beamed, happy to add years to an age he obviously didn't approve of. 'Come December,' she admitted, less happily but more truthfully.

'Twenty-two, in other words,' Jason corrected.

'Yes, sir,' she admitted soberly, bobbing her head and watching him through the veil of her lowered lashes. He was not impressed, not impressed at all. She experienced a sinking feeling in the pit of her stomach. He knew more about her than she did about him and had no intention of letting her turn the tables.

'A child surrounded by a house full of children,' he accused.

'No, sir,' Katie shook her head vehemently. That matter had been taken to court and settled. Her parents' wills, naming her guardian of all minor children and distributor of all their property, real and personal, were unusual but valid. She had been since the age of eighteen, by court order, a responsible adult. 'I am their legal guardian.'

Her spirited denial raised a sceptical eyebrow. 'How many brothers do you have, Miss Staunton?'

Katie had hoped that that question wouldn't come up. Even Miss Hawk, the social worker and a stickler for rules and regulations, remained voluntarily blind to the fact that there were four boys where there should have been only three. Squaring her shoulders, Katie stared at her folded hands.

'Three, sir.' Quickly she buried the three fingers that had popped up to affirm her answer and dragged them back to her lap.

'I count four.' With a hint of a smile, Jason raised his hand, four fingers spread, thumb tucked under.

'Yes, sir.' Katie forced her eyes to meet his. If he wanted to know more he would just have to ask!

He outwaited her by simply crossing his arms and looking at her, or rather through her. His eyes were the azure of an October sky and his face might have been carved from the stone of her hills.

'Rocky is a school friend visiting for a few days,' she lied, dragging her eyes back to her lap. Peeping up at him, she realised he knew better than that. 'He lives here. He's one of us,' she admitted. 'Rocky's our cousin. His father is working in the Oklahoma oilfields.'

Randall Jackson was a cousin if family history was traced back far enough. Go back to Adam and Eve and everybody was a cousin. And his father had been in the Oklahoma fields six months ago. She didn't know that he wasn't still there. Rocky was a child in need of a home and Katie had home and heart large enough to house him. Nothing else was needed.

'I see,' Jason raised his hand again, thumb and little finger tucked under. 'You have three brothers, legally yours.' The little finger sprang erect. 'And friend, not so legally yours.' The thumb rose to greet its fellow fingers. 'And now Alicia. You propose to care for five children?'

'Yes, sir.' Five, ten, an even dozen, it wouldn't have made any difference. There was always room for one more.

'In a house ready to fall down around your ears?'

The panther pounced with practised skill, rising from his perch on the edge of the desk to stalk her from a distance that wasn't nearly far enough away.

'No, sir.' Resisting the urge to crawl inside the chair and hide, Katie sat up even straighter, ready to defend herself and her home. 'The house is structurally sound, as sound as the day it was built. There are no termites and no leaks.' She hid her left hand under her right elbow and double-crossed her fingers to protect against him discovering the slight untruth she was about to speak. 'Mr Selby is going to scrape and repaint the trim, come September, which it truly does need, if he can work us in.' Repainting the trim and shutters wasn't a question of Jake Selby's time, it was a matter of her money.

'The roof leaks.' Jason pursued the house's faults relentlessly, coming even closer as he did.

'No, sir.' Katie denied his accusation with a quick shake of her head and looked for something less disturbing than him to look at. The mismatched shingles had cost her dearly in coin silver serving pieces and a set of cut glass salts, discreetly sold through Hank Felton. 'The roof is patched, but it doesn't leak,' she told the wall.

'Your driveway is an obstacle course.'

'The lane does need a bit of smoothing.' She smoothed over what the brood referred to as the craters of the moon with a sweep of her hand.

'I suppose Mr Selby will smooth a bit when he paints a bit,' drawled Jason, scepticism creeping into his voice.

'No, sir,' Katie vowed, his caustic tone stinging her pride. 'I planned to have that done by the end of the month. The rains will be pretty much over by then.' She recrossed her fingers just to be safe. Bobby Ray Spencer was always looking for some excuse to come around. She'd flutter her lashes and simper a bit and feel guilty about using him and his father's tractor, later, when she had time.

'I see.'

Katie had the uncomfortable feeling that he did see, more than she wanted him to see.

Jason paced the room, stopping to pull one of the Legislative Reviews from its shelf. He flipped aimlessly through the pages before shutting it with a snap. 'Your grandfather was a moonshiner,' he accused.

'No, sir.'

'No, sir?' His eyes flickered over her in a chilly rebuttal. That fact was very clear. Criminal convictions were a matter of public record.

'No, sir,' Katie spat, thrusting her chin forward and glaring just as angrily. When she said yes she meant yes. When she said no she meant no. It wasn't her fault he didn't know how to ask precise questions. 'No Staunton has ever made bootleg whisky for sale.'

'Made for sale?' Jason scoffed. 'That's a rather narrow distinction, isn't it? Ah, but then you're also the lawyer's daughter. I forgot. Very well, lawyer's daughter, your grandfather transported illegal alcohol.' He bowed his head in mocking deference, but not before Katie saw amusement lurking in his eyes and tugging at his firmly chiselled mouth.

'Yes, sir.' She clamped her lips tightly together to keep any further information from leaking out. He was altogether too clever and pleased with himself as it was.

'While his brother was sheriff? That was a cosy arrangement?'

'No, sir, not cosy at all,' Katie snapped. 'If it had been cosy he wouldn't have gotten caught. My grandfather never denied or made any excuses for what he did. And Uncle Bo never looked the other way for him. They had babies to feed and taxes to pay. They burned their corn for firewood rather than sell it for two cents a bushel. Those were hard times, and they did what was necessary to survive.' Anger and pride deepened her voice to a husky whisper.

'Necessity?' Jason's raised eyebrow formed an arrogant question mark. 'And out of necessity you worked the bar at Tara?'

'I didn't work the bar! Prostitutes work bars,' Katie hissed angrily, green fire igniting and flashing in her narrowed eyes. His contempt turned an occupation that was little more than glorified waitressing in short shorts into something unclean. 'I worked in a bar, yes, for three whole months. For money, necessary money.'

Pasting a smile over her anger, she stood, balancing a drink tray in her left hand. Gracefully she slid past him, demonstrating the quick sideways turn that had allowed her to move through a maze of closely packed tables without bumping customers or dumping drinks. She handed him an imaginary drink. 'Why, thank you, sir.' Her playful smile hardened. 'Next time tip a little more, Mr Reese. Your waitress may be working for the money, not just the pleasure of your company.

'Toting drinks is easy. All you have to do is smile and sidestep the pinches and propositions for ten hours a day. Try it some time, I'm sure you'll like it. But don't forget to smile. When you tell that married fool in the corner to go to hell, do it nice—and smile. You need his tip and the boss wants him to come back tomorrow.'

Temper and stinging pride overrode Katie's common sense, warning her to keep a distance. As she advanced on him, her eyes smouldered with memories of men who considered cocktail waitresses as nothing more than amateur prostitutes bought with the price of a drink.

'I've done nothing to be ashamed of doing. I don't owe you or anybody else an explanation or an apology for my life. Do you have any more questions?' she demanded with a proud toss of her head.

'Yes, as a matter of fact, I do.' His eyes glittered with

something akin to admiration for the defiant girl who refused to be pitied or beaten. 'As I understand it, you now propose to support this'—his hand swept the room and the house beyond—'establishment of children by peddling strawberries?'

'No, sir, I don't propose to do so, I have done so for four years now and will continue to do so as long as necessary. It's legal and it pays the bills.' Triumphantly, she swept past him and opened her drop-front desk. 'Would you care to examine my books?'

'I believe that's already been done.' Jason bowed his dark head towards her, acknowledging her victory over Miss Hawk and her claim of mismanagement in their second legal battle.

'You had me checked out!' Katie spluttered.

'Of course, this afternoon. Something that should have been done when my aunt first suggested you.' Cool blue eyes devoid of guilt bored into her brain. 'To be perfectly honest, Miss Staunton, my objections have nothing to do with the care you gave Alicia. It was adequate, more than adequate. I object to you. You don't even have enough sense to know that you can't possibly succeed at this.' He shook his head, despairing her many follies. 'I expected to find a rational, middle-aged widow, and instead I find a disorganised, impulsive child who explores attics and digs up dancing floors while forgetting to buy shoes.'

Katie ducked her head and the undeniable accusation being flung at her. He could have also added stiff-necked and hard-headed. She didn't blame him. He could now say that he had tried but it was an impossible situation.

'No matter,' Jason sighed, clawing at his thick walnut-brown hair and wondering if he wasn't being just as foolish and impulsive. 'Whatever your shortcomings, you're good with children, very good—perhaps because you're one yourself. And that's all I

require. If I removed Alicia from your care it would be
for personal reasons, not because I thought it best for
her.'

'And if I refused to keep her it would be for personal
reasons and not because I thought it best for her,'
huffed Katie, her fears of losing Poppet lost in her
renewed irritation. Child! Shortcomings! 'But,' she
continued, mimicking his thoughtful phrasing and cool
tone, 'we are both adults. It would be foolish to allow
our mutual dislike to hurt Poppet.'

Jason nodded, not bothering to mouth the polite
disclaimers convention required.

'There's one other thing, Miss Staunton. My time
with Alicia is already more limited than I like. I need a
room.'

'Of course.' Katie covered her surprise with a casual
shrug and ignored that part of her mind no longer
preoccupied with being angry and warning her against
allowing this dangerously masculine stranger into her
home and life. Her eyes wandered to his firmly muscled
chest and shoulders broad enough to lean on before she
jerked them away. He was Poppet's father, and this was
business.

'I have fourteen rooms in this house, seven of them
bedrooms. You can have your pick of the empty ones
. . . At a price,' some imp made her add.

'How much?'

'Twenty dollars.' She grabbed the first number that
floated through her mind. 'That's a month and includes
meals,' her shocked sense of hospitality insisted.

'That seems very reasonable.'

'Yes, sir,' Katie mumbled. She peeped at him through
her lashes. He was waiting. He meant now. 'I'll show
you the way,' she offered.

Quietly thoughtful, she led the way back to the living
room. She had the feeling that somehow she had just
been bested, a feeling she wasn't used to experiencing.

A stair-step of five guilty-looking children leered at them from the turn of the stairs.

'Got Poppet all settled,' Jeeter volunteered.

'Fine.' Katie bobbed her head, not fully aware of who had said what. 'Mr Reese is staying too.'

'Daddy!' squealed Poppet, tumbling down the stairs to pull him up.

The boys slipped into the background. Poppet they wanted. Him they would watch and then make their decision.

Katie pushed open the door to the second of the west bedrooms, the one not directly opposite hers. 'I think this one would be the best, Mr Reese.'

She allowed herself to gloat just a little. The bedrooms were as high-ceilinged and spacious as the first-floor rooms. The massive furniture in this room was all matching walnut, and the bed was a masterpiece. Its square, carved headboard rose to a height of eight feet and the footboard was a respectable four feet high, solid walnut.

'It'll do fine,' Jason agreed, not really looking.

'Bathrooms at either end of the hall,' house-proud Katie informed him tersely.

'Come and see my room, Daddy.' Poppet tugged at his hand and shot an anxious look at Katie.

She led her father across the hall to the room that was nominally hers. She pointed out the handkerchief drawers and candle stands on the dressing table, hinting to him that such things were important to Katie. Then she got down to the important stuff, treasure. Solemnly, one by one, she handed him the bits and pieces she and Jeeter had discovered; wren egg, robin egg, fossilised shell, blue jay feather, a chunk of twisted tree root polished smooth by the water they had rescued it from, a bent square nail. Much to Katie's relief, he recognised their worth to young eyes still open wide enough to find treasure in every moment and handled them just as reverently.

Returning the nail to its proper position at precisely the correct angle, Poppet bobbed her head and dusted her hands, as Katie did when she felt something was done and done well.

'I don't sleep in here, though, I sleep with Katie. She's afraid of the dark. That's one of the reasons why she was so glad when I came, she doesn't have to sleep alone any more,' Poppet announced, pulling her mouth into a tight bud, making sure that her father realised that this was just one of many reasons why she should stay.

'I see,' Jason answered gravely, while Katie studied the interesting grooves in the floorboards. She sensed that he knew as well as she did who was afraid of the dark and that he would no more betray his daughter's secret than she would.

'Wait till you see our bed,' Poppet bragged happily. 'It's a marriage bed, isn't it, Katie?'

'Mr Reese, have you had supper yet?' Katie interjected before Poppet could continue the house tour to the next room.

'Yes, we have.'

'We were about to have dessert. Wouldn't you like some dessert? Strawberries and ice cream,' Katie pleaded.

Jason swung Poppet up in his arms and gently poked at her rounded tummy. 'I thought so—an empty spot! Were you saving that for something special?'

'Yes,' giggled Poppet, forgetting the marriage bed in her enjoyment of their private game. 'Strawberries. Our strawberries, Daddy,' she whispered, wrapping her arms around his neck.

'It would be our pleasure to join you for dessert, Miss Staunton,' answered Jason, the light dancing in his eyes at odds with his formal acceptance.

'Yes, sir.'

Ducking her head, Katie retreated, pretending she didn't know he was following.

In the kitchen her hands went about their business of dishing up ice cream while her mind skittered here and there. He simply wasn't conforming to her notion of what a Jason Reese should be.

Her reaction to him wasn't exactly what she'd thought it would be either, but then it hadn't exactly been a normal day, with the boys—the boys! Grabbing two bowls of ice cream, she turned to face the ominously quiet crowd in the kitchen.

'Guests first,' she smiled. 'It'll be cooler outside, there's a good breeze coming up.' Still smiling stiffly at Jason and Poppet, she shot the boys a silent warning; if they were considering a little devilry they'd better unconsider, fast. Lacing Bobby Ray Spencer's strawberries with hot pepper sauce was one thing, attempting the same thing with Jason Reese would be an entirely different proposition.

'The dancing floor and my playhouse, Daddy,' Poppet chirped, remembering that he had seen neither.

Breathing a sigh of relief at their backs, Katie handed around the rest of the ice cream. 'Manners!' she hissed, jerking her head towards the back door.

They sat in uncomfortable silence, Jason and Poppet in the wicker settee, Katie on the ground opposite them, her bare feet tucked under her, and the boys in a scowling but mannerly semi-circle behind her. Katie knew she should say something. She had learned the art of pleasant small talk early. Her father had been a gregarious man even before he had entered public life and the house had often overflowed with guests, guests Katie had routinely charmed. But she couldn't think of one charming thing to say, so she said nothing. Instead she ate her ice cream slowly and hoped it would last until full dark when she could remember that they had to get up early and therefore had to go to bed early.

Tonguetied as she was, her eyes kept a veiled watch on the two of them. Poppet was nestled close to his side, her hand claiming the strength of his, her drooping head not quite concealing a pouting underlip.

Breathing in sharply, Katie silently berated herself for being so blind and small-hearted. Screaming at the top of their lungs wouldn't have been any more hostile than their silence. The screeching silence told Poppet that she could have her father or them, but she could not have both. Their very alignment in opposing camps made it all too plain to her that they were wary combatants. That was too heavy a burden for any child to bear, and even worse, the blame was Katie's. She had become so engrossed with her reaction to Jason Reese, the man, and how she might avoid him, she had played tug-of-war with a child's feelings.

'It seems my eyes were bigger than my stomach,' Katie fibbed, setting her uneaten ice cream aside. She paused, a pained smile on her face. She really had nothing else to say.

'Mr Reese, perhaps you would like to see our visible means of support, the strawberry bed.' Her smile softened into genuine delight as she gracefully uncoiled from her seat on the ground. She could safely keep the conversation on strawberries for as long as necessary. She could tell him everything he ever wanted to know about the care and cultivation of strawberries and more.

Her hand at her side, she furtively waved the boys to follow. Not only did she require their moral support, she wanted to know exactly where they were and what they were doing.

Showing the neat strawberry bed didn't take as long as Katie hoped. Explaining that each plant was allowed to set only one runner and that at the end of the season the old plants were dug out to keep the bed young and vigorous didn't take long either. Pests and diseases, storage and marketing were all covered just as swiftly, leaving Katie once more with nothing to say.

'We get seven per cent above market,' Jeeter boasted proudly. ''Cause we're the best.'

'A quality produce should receive a premium,' Jason congratulated, causing the boy's chest to swell until Katie's chilly look and Chance's fingers hooking and twisting the belt loops on the waistband of his jeans reminded him that bragging was unmannerly.

'Come and see my playhouse,' inserted Poppet, pushing away the silence threatening to engulf them.

With the sure instincts of a vulture or a healthy child, she swooped down on Jeeter, the weak brick in the wall of silence, to drag him along. Jeeter complied, aided by a mannerly shove from the rear. Katie, darting a glance of disapproval at the remaining boys, followed.

'This was originally the wash-house,' she explained when they had entered the small stone building that was half porch and several yards from the back of the main house.

'They used to boil their laundry. They didn't have electricity,' Poppet added two details which had most amazed her.

'Yup.' Using a discarded canoe paddle, Jeeter stirred the empty six-foot-diameter cast-iron cauldron permanently cemented into a brick firebox that took up the entire back wall.

'But it's been a playhouse for years and years now and it's so glad there's a little girl here again. It's been lonesome all by itself. Isn't that right, Katie?' Poppet coached.

'Yes, that's right,' Katie agreed softly, even though she knew Jason Reese was too adult to believe that a building or any other inanimate object could be lonesome. She knew Poppet wasn't that grown up and, in truth, neither was she.

'I don't think I've ever seen a finer playhouse.' Jason

nodded gravely, looking around the little house and adding to himself, or so much love so willingly shared.

'And everything is just Poppet-sized,' added Poppet, settling into a perfectly scaled down rocking chair that had been brought down from the attic that morning. 'We get to have tea parties and everything, but no fires.'

'That's because Bo and Rocky blew up their lab,' Jeeter grumbled.

'They did,' Poppet echoed in the face of Jason's rising disbelief.

'Blew the windows right out of the frames,' Jeeter detailed proudly before realising his mistake. 'But Katie told them if it ever happened again and they didn't kill themselves she would. Made them pay for the windows too.'

Ducking Katie's unsoothed displeasure, he returned to stirring the cauldron.

'Is this lab still in operation?' Jason asked in a deceptively quiet tone that didn't deceive Katie for one minute.

'Yes, sir,' admitted Katie, wishing Jeeter had never learned to talk. 'They're normally very careful. The chemicals were mislabelled—I have a letter from the company that says as much.'

'Daddy, come and see the dancing floor!' Poppet tugging at his hand reclaimed Jason's attention.

Katie was given a few much needed moments of peace while Poppet pulled Jason here and there, explaining that tomorrow, with more light, he could see initials and even full names and dates carved into some of the paving stones. As she listened to Poppet playing the charming hostess, Katie closed her eyes and begged that no more little family secrets be divulged tonight—a plea which she soon discovered had been ignored. By the time she realised their voices had drifted from the part of the dancing floor that had been cleared and that the conversation had also drifted, it was too late.

'And there used to be a summer kitchen, Daddy, right here.' Poppet drew a rectangle in the air roughly outlining the perimeter of the demolished summer kitchen.

'Till Grandpa Staunton ran over it,' Jeeter volunteered.

'He forgot he was driving an automobile instead of a horse. When he hollered, "Whoa!" it didn't stop,' Poppet recited, quoting from one of the many tales Katie loved to tell and they loved to hear.

'Knocked the whole front wall down.'

'Tore off the porch too.'

'Didn't do the car much good neither,' Jeeter added straight-faced.

'I—er—suppose not,' Jason concurred soberly, scrubbing his mouth with the side of his hand, scrubbing away the smile he sensed Katie was incapable of appreciating at the moment.

'By the time you boys get your baths taken it'll be bedtime,' Katie announced. The tilt of her chin and the crisp tone of her voice warning that arguments were not only unwelcome but possibly unhealthy.

The boys safely stashed at their end of the house, Katie pulled sheets and pillowcases from the double wardrobe in the hall that served as a linen closet. While Jason was telling Poppet goodnight she would make up his bed and make sure the slats were still under the springs where they belonged.

Her arms full of bedlinen, Katie paused to smile and shake her head. Poppet was still talking a mile a minute, trying to tell her daddy everything at once. The child's joy in her father being with her made all else secondary.

CHAPTER THREE

MORE asleep than awake, Katie sensed a difference—something was missing. Her mind stumbled out of sleep and into panic. There was no Poppet cuddled up to her, no Poppet in the bed.

A hasty but thorough search of Katie's bedroom and the adjoining room where Poppet kept her treasures and clothes failed to produce the little one. Katie raked a shaking hand through her sleep-tousled hair. Where could she have gone? The alarm hadn't rung and the child normally had to be pried out of bed in the morning. She'd never had this happen before, but she knew she couldn't very well knock on Jason's bedroom door and say, 'Excuse me, sir, but it seems I've lost your child.' Not after yesterday.

The rabbit. Katie slumped against the bedpost, relief pouring through her. Chance had given Poppet a baby wild rabbit which they had tamed. Poppet whispered most of her secrets and important news in the little cottontail's long ears; she might have gone down to the pen to tell the rabbit all the news.

Not wanting to waste the precious time it would take to dress, Katie tiptoed into the hallway wearing only her cotton nightshirt, selected mostly for warm weather comfort. The soft murmur of two voices brushed her ear. Through the partially open door of Jason's bedroom she saw Poppet astride his bare chest. She was telling her favourite of the many tales Katie loved to spin, how in 1853 John Staunton had gone to New Orleans looking for adventure and a hat for his mother and come back a year later with the hat and the hatmaker, his bride. The family Bible listed her as

Marie Claude Devereaux, but she was remembered as the Louisiana Bride, and it was her bed, fetched upriver and overland from New Orleans, that Katie and Poppet slept on.

His attention was focused on Poppet tying the strings of John Staunton's mama's new hat under her chin. Jason straightened the bonnet on her blonde head, his hand lingering to cup her chin and tilt her head to better study the effect of the non-existent hat. Ashamed of what amounted to eavesdropping, Katie stepped away from the open door. Whatever had separated Jason Reese from his daughter, it wasn't lack of caring; the depth of his caring was reflected in his absorption in her tale and his gentle touch. She had no right to intrude on their time together.

Her movement caught his attention, which in turn caused Poppet to twist around to see what was so interesting behind her.

'Katie, John Staunton did so go to New Orleans in 1854, didn't he?'

'In 1853—he came back in 1854.'

'And he did bring the Louisiana Bride back with him, didn't he?'

'Yes.'

'And your bed is her bed, ain't it?'

'Isn't it,' Katie corrected automatically. 'Yes, it is.'

'And you are going to have your babies in that bed?'

'I plan to have my babies in hospital,' Katie parried, not liking the turn the conversation had taken.

Poppet threw her a look of pure exasperation. She was not in a mood to appreciate word games. 'Well, they're going to sleep in the cradle.'

'When the time comes,' Katie admitted, her face warming. The cradle that had sheltered several generations of Stauntons had been discovered in the attic along with the playhouse furniture. Katie being Katie had told Poppet the tale of the cradle, and Poppet being Poppet had wanted to know if Katie's babies were going to use it too. It was one thing to daydream with Poppet, quite another to have those daydreams paraded for his cool evaluation.

Poppet grinned triumphantly and bowed her fair head towards her father, as if to say—There, I told you so.

'Is it time to get up, Katie?'

'Not yet, you still have time to talk.'

Her mind already skipping past Katie's answer, Poppet slid from her lofty perch. 'I help Katie with the accounts. Accounts are very important. If we don't keep our records straight we don't get paid.'

'A sound business practice,' her father agreed solemnly. An indulgent smile toyed with his firm mouth, reaching up to crinkle the corners of his deep-set eyes. 'Get dressed, then you can show me your rabbit.' A hug and a kiss hurried Poppet on her way.

'I'd like a word with you, Miss Staunton,' announced Jason before Katie could also disappear. 'Are you getting married soon?'

'No, sir.' Katie shook her head to reinforce her answer. Any softness, any human emotion the man might have felt seemed to have left the room with his child.

'Well then, is there, shall we say, a special young man in your life?'

'No, sir.' Katie felt her face warm under his chilly appraisal. Discounting Bobby Ray Spencer, and she'd been discounting him for years, there was no man in her life over the age of fifteen. She squared her slight shoulders and glared at him. Anything more was none of his business.

She jerked her eyes to a point above the top of the window, her face flaming. Mr Jason Reese was not a believer in pyjamas. Not that she had been purposely looking. It was hard to miss when a man was wearing little more than a sheet.

'Is something wrong, Miss Staunton?'

'No, sir,' Katie insisted, the memory of his bare chest and the outline of firm masculine hips and thighs moulding the sheets shaking her senses and voice.

'I understand that you're a normal, healthy young woman with normal, healthy desires, but I believe I'm well within my rights to ask that you keep your relationships discreet.'

'Well, I don't!' Katie managed to gasp, spinning on her heel for a dignified exit. Realising that her answer could be misconstrued several ways, she spun back around and faced him with blazing green anger snapping in her eyes. 'I don't indulge in relationships, discreet or otherwise. I'm worth more than that—to me. And while we're discussing discretion, Mr Reese, what you do in the privacy of your own room is your affair, as long as you're discreet. But when you step beyond this door I must insist that you be fully dressed. It's a house rule.'

His mouth quirked into a devilish grin as his eyes made a leisurely assessment of her thin nightgown and the soft curves the translucent material loosely veiled.

'Yes, sir,' Katie insisted, her face flaming once more as she fled to the safety of her own room.

She sat down on the edge of her bed with a thump, her legs too shaky to bear her weight any longer. 'The gall of that man!' she spluttered. 'Sitting there naked as a jaybird or near enough, spouting his normals and healthies and getting an eyeful the whole time!'

She hid her burning face in her hands. What was the man to think, except that he'd landed in a nest of half-witted lunatics. What with shoeless daughters being kidnapped and finding a family tree dripping with summer-kitchen-destroying bootleggers and barmaids, he was well within his rights to be a mite uncivil. Considering the fact that she'd been prancing around in a nightshirt so thin and worn as to make a sheet look as solid as a brick wall in comparison, he hadn't even been uncivil.

There'd be no more of that, Katie vowed silently. She'd be as prim and proper as an old maid schoolteacher. So cool and businesslike he'd have to see her in a better light—for Poppet's sake, of course.

A fully dressed Poppet burst through the connecting door, a whirlwind of joyful excitement. She threw herself at Katie and crushed her in a bear hug that sent them both tumbling backwards.

'Do you like my daddy?'

'How could I not like your daddy?' hedged Katie, her heart quivering with the knowledge that the turmoil she was experiencing had nothing to do with Poppet. She kissed the little one and patted her rump to speed her on her way reassured.

From the window Katie watched a giggling, chattering Poppet pull Jason along through the dew-laden grass to the rabbit pen.

'There does seem to be a problem here, girl,' she murmured, allowing the curtain to fall back in place.

The problem was shoved to a far corner of her mind by the sound of ringing alarm clocks and sleepy moans. There were strawberries to be delivered, a whole day waiting for her, and she wasn't even dressed.

The morning routine was so well established no one noticed that Katie was late or commented on the fact that she was wearing mint green dress slacks instead of jeans and a long-sleeved, loose-fitting, matching striped top, buttoned up to her chin. She checked the arrangement of racks of berries filling the area behind the second seat of the Bronco, a cross between a station wagon and a four-wheel-drive pick-up. The berries were all in proper order following the delivery route. The three older boys were in the back seat, Jeeter positioned by the passenger door and Poppet in the middle of the front seat, sitting on Jason's lap.

'Daddy's coming too,' Poppet informed Katie.

Katie forced her mouth to smile and bobbed her head. He certainly was, every male inch and ounce of him. There had to be some way of getting him out of there, gracefully, tactfully. 'I think—er—I——' Katie stammered. 'It's illegal to have four people in the front seat.'

'I gotta be by a door so I can open doors,' Jeeter, fearful of loosing his honoured position by a window, reminded her.

'But I'm not sitting on the seat, Katie, I'm sitting on Daddy,' Poppet reasoned sweetly.

'Good point,' smiled Katie, doubting the validity of Poppet's argument but not willing to challenge it.

For a few minutes Katie had a perfectly legitimate excuse to ignore Jason. The strawberries were stored overnight in the spring house, a natural refrigerator. In the evenings Katie backed the truck close to the spring house door, handy for the morning's loading. Bringing the truck in or out of the area of the spring house was a touchy proposition. Grandpa Staunton might have been the only one to actually run over a building, but a close examination would show that his wasn't the only vehicle which had become intimately acquainted with various objects.

After the truck had been successfully manoeuvred around buildings, trees, stumps and holes to the beginning of the lane, Katie did as she always did— blew a sigh of relief and leaned her head against the back of the seat. She knew it was only a matter of time and luck; sooner or later she had to miscalculate and hit something. Jerking upright, she realised it wasn't the seat her neck was touching, but the living warmth of Jason's arm casually draped along the back of the seat. Her eyes slid in his direction just as her foot hit the gas pedal. Unguided, the truck lurched forward through a large but shallow puddle. Jerking her eyes and mind back to driving, Katie managed to put only three wheels into the next hole, nicknamed 'The Whopper'.

'Woo-whee! You got two at one go that time, Katie!' someone in the back seat whooped. She rarely hit a chuck-hole, and when she did highly vocal encouragement was always given.

Her foot firmly on the brake, Katie first peeped at Jason. He didn't appear to think that anything out of the ordinary had happened. 'Everybody all right?'

'Yes, ma'am.' They recognised the tone and look being reflected at them through the rear-view mirror. If death wasn't imminent, there were no injuries worth mentioning.

Exercising great care and total concentration, Katie eased the truck along the lane. At the far end, waiting for a car to pass by, she unbuttoned the top two buttons of her blouse. She was warm, she assured herself, only because it was an unusually hot morning.

Katie's tensions eased as the morning wore on. Everything was going normally. At each stop she backed the truck as close to the delivery entrance as possible. As soon as the truck stopped, Jeeter jumped out and raced to the delivery door and took up his duty as door opener. Katie and Chance handed down filled trays and returned empties. Bo and Rocky toted and Poppet proudly marked off each stop in turn. A few minutes were always spent at each stop discussing world-shaking events and current gossip. Even though there were a great many craning necks and wondering looks no one asked who the man in the truck was, and Katie felt no compelling urge to enlighten them.

The last stop was Tara and Joseph Tarrel. Joseph's father, Cletus Tarrel, had stopped by Cousin John Staunton's in the late twenties, hoping to find work for his strong back and ready hands at the Bagnall Dam hydro-electric project. He'd stayed because he had a mind that could not only see what was, but what could be, and raised his family on that vision—Tara, a self-contained resort complex worthy of its setting. The old man had dreamed and his five sons had made it come true. Joseph, the youngest of the sons, ruled Tara's kitchens.

Joseph Tarrel seldom missed the arrival of his favourite delivery crew. The title of cousin, which even in the old men's day had been diluted to more courtesy than kinship, had been discarded in his boyhood. Neither he nor Tommie Staunton had needed it. Their strong friendship had been enough. Each had stood as godfather to the other's firstborn. At times Joseph considered his goddaughter exasperating, too full of prickly pride and independence to be sensible. But knowing her parents and grandparents he realised she couldn't be any other way. So he hovered in the background, doing what he could do for the orphans, which consisted mostly of worrying and offering free caramel rolls still warm from the oven.

'Who's that?' he asked Katie, exercising his self-given right to oversee her life—a right Katie could never in a million years convince him he didn't have.

'Poppet's father,' she muttered, passing along another tray of berries.

'That right?' Joseph drawled under his breath, stretching his short thick body to get a better view of the front seat. 'I thought there for a minute maybe you'd found yourself a husband.'

'When I need a husband, I'll let you know!' Katie hissed, her eyes flashing her irritation with their long-running, teasing argument which had lost all its humour this morning.

'You need one,' retorted Joseph, enjoying the spark of temper he'd ignited. Hitching up his breeches, he jerked his head towards the front seat and Poppet. 'Since there's no living with you this morning, maybe I'll go see if my little darling still loves me.'

While Katie and the boys finished with the strawberries, Joseph struck up a conversation Katie couldn't quite hear. When he waved them goodbye the speculative gleam in his eye was all too easy to understand.

Deciding it was stupid to swelter, Katie changed into her everyday shorts before breakfast. Not that anyone noticed; they were all too busy planning all that they wanted Jason to see and to do to look at Katie or notice that she was unnaturally quiet. Including him. She might just as well have been a robot passing platters of food and asking if he wanted more coffee. When the final plans were announced, Katie nodded and agreed and told herself that she was glad he wasn't going to be underfoot all day.

The table cleared, the quiet kitchen was too quiet and too empty. Katie watched as Bo and Rocky led the way to their lab, half of an unused machine shed. Poppet was riding on Jason's shoulder, one arm wrapped around his head, her free hand making a sweep of the hollow that contained the house and was the centre of Katie's world. The boys were a surging, chattering circle surrounding him, vying for and enjoying the warmth of his attention. Even the hills seemed to be bending closer, smiling down on him.

Sniffing her disgust for such a lunatic notion, Katie plunged her hands into the waiting dishwater, but the problem of Jason Reese and what to do wasn't that easily dismissed. Maybe the hills weren't trembling because he was there, but she was. Just thinking about him had almost the same effect as being near him. She had listened to her friends discuss such feelings before and had always dismissed the chatter as so much wistful dreaming. Now she wasn't so sure.

What can't be cured must be endured—one of her Grandma Staunton's favourite sayings popped into her mind. Since she had no intention of enduring that left only curing, because attracted and distracted she certainly was. But then, she reasoned, Jason was a compellingly attractive man and she wasn't dead, the only condition capable of rendering a woman immune to his excitingly masculine presence. Her racing pulse had done nothing more than react to the intuitively feminine knowledge that in him was power and possible danger, and that was what had been making the world go around since Adam and Eve ate the apple.

Her temporary lack of resistance was not only natural but excusable, she further reasoned. The shock of finding this Jason Reese on her doorstep and not the contemptible little man she had imagined him to be had lowered her resistance. The episode with the boys kidnapping Poppet and threatening to shoot him certainly hadn't helped either. Then Joseph yammering about husbands had made her even more susceptible.

But it was curable, she assured herself. It was a condition akin to catching a cold and having it turn into pneumonia because you walked in the rain. Curing pneumonia was simple, you simply got out of the rain and went to a doctor and got a prescription for penicillin. For man fever what? Anti-man serum? Doctors had no such thing. What she needed then was a little home-made anti-man serum. Like that old home remedy, whisky and honey, which could cure a cold before it turned into pneumonia, distance and people, carefully measured and adhered to, could cure her of attraction before it turned into man fever.

With a confident bob of her head, Dr Kathleen Staunton prescribed ten feet and/or two children between them at all times. Considering that there were five children underfoot and a large house and garden also demanding her attention, she saw no problem maintaining that dosage. She was also certain that given time her good common sense would regain its strength and effect a permanent cure.

The fact that this particular virus, if Jason could be called that, had no interest in attacking also helped. Her pride was naturally stung; most men found her desirable and made no secret of it. He didn't. It was as simple as that, and considering her weakened condition, most fortunate. If yesterday hadn't made his lack of interest plain enough, today had. Relationships! Discretion! Not only did he consider her a barefoot, dirty-faced hillbilly child, he considered her a none too moral one at that. Katie added righteous indignation to her prescription.

The effectiveness of her prescription was tested shortly after lunch.

Jeeter and Poppet thundered into the kitchen to make their breathless announcement. Chance was taking Jay fishing and they were invited to join the fishing party. Katie bit back a smile and suggested that maybe the fishermen should be locating fishing poles and tackle unless they were planning to hypnotise the fish into jumping in the pan.

'Katie,' Jeeter hissed. Too intent on his own thoughts to laugh at hers, he motioned her down to his eye level. 'If we catch 'em you will cook 'em, won't you?'

'Boy, anything you can catch and clean I can cook.' Eyes sparkling, Katie tugged the end of the boy's freckled snub nose and made a face at him. 'Now, what do you really have on that beady little mind of yours?'

'Hush-puppies.'

Growling a completely non-threatening growl deep in her throat, Katie dived for his ticklish ribs. 'Whoever heard of a fish fry without hush-puppies?'

Poppet, not wanting to be left out of the fun, wriggled into the magic circle of Katie's arms. 'What are hush-puppies?'

'Why, child,' Katie drawled in her best story-telling drawl as she wrapped an arm around each child and pulled them both to the floor to sit on either side of her, 'we have neglected your education. Hush-puppies are little balls of deep fried corn bread, more or less. About so big around.' She made a circle with her thumb and forefinger. 'Rumour has it that the hunters out on a hunting trip used to make them for supper and then throw the leftovers to the dogs and say, "Hush, puppy." That's the legend, anyway. Maybe that's why hunting dogs are so skinny—there are never any left over.' Laughing, she dragged the tip of her finger across Poppet's wrinkled nose. 'They're good. You have to eat them when they're so hot all you can do is bounce them from hand to hand to cool them down.'

She demonstrated how a hungry hush-puppy eater juggled the steaming hot titbits.

'You gotta grab 'em when they're hot, 'cause if you don't somebody else will,' Jeeter continued for her. 'Then you break 'em open and slather 'em down with honey and butter and eat the whole thing in one big bite.' He caressed his lips with the tip of his tongue and rubbed his belly.

'Um-m-m,' Katie agreed. Standing and pulling them to their feet, she gave each a squeezing hug of thanks for returning her joy in living to her. They were powerful medicine indeed.

'But first you have to catch the fish and clean them. You'll notice that I said catch and clean. You clean, I cook. But first you have to catch them, so you'd best get going.'

'Ah, Katie! We're going to catch so many fish you'll have to call in half the county just to eat 'em all,' Jeeter bragged.

'You just do that, boy,' challenged Katie, ruffling his hair that no amount of combing could tame.

When the excited pair had taken their giggles and high expectations off to locate fishing rods a prickling sensation walking down her spine alerted Katie to the fact that she wasn't alone. With a proud toss of her head, she turned to face Jason. That he had seen and heard and considered this just one more example of her childish nature was visible in the smile twitching the corners of his mouth.

'If being an adult means that you expect me to run around with a sour face pretending that I don't enjoy what I do enjoy, I hope I never grow up,' she told him. 'Fact is, I've often thought that the world would be a much better place if we sent the adults out to play their games and let the children run things.'

'That's an interesting theory,' Jason admitted, his smile growing lopsided and softening the harsh lines of his face in a way that sent Katie's heart crashing against her ribs.

'Yes, sir,' she muttered, moving out of range of his disturbing influence on her racing pulse, concentrating on the green beans she was washing and tipping.

He draped his long frame over a chair and watched her with an intensity that negated her carefully plotted distance.

'I'm not in the habit of keeping fishing rods in the kitchen, Mr Reese.' Keeping her back to him, Katie invited him to leave.

'Kathleen, I believe you misunderstood what I said this morning.'

Katie stabbed a green bean and scowled at its rusty tip and thought about how much she had hated picking green beans when she was a child. Beans had to be picked in the heat of the day, after the dew had burned off or they rusted. She chopped off the rusty end. He had left no room for even one little misunderstanding. There had been no rust on his words.

'I meant that you needed a day or evening off duty now and then.'

'No, sir, that is not what you meant,' Katie contradicted with a haughty lift of her chin.

'That's what I should have meant.'

A small flutter of pleasure stirred her. That was the nicest apology she'd ever heard. She hid her pleasure with a careless shrug and kept the corners of her mouth turned down in a pouting frown.

'Kathleen, my friends call me Jay.'

'Yes, sir,' she admitted warily, fearing what he was going to say. He was already Jay to the brood. They had spent the entire morning entertaining him. Their labours went beyond making amends, even the desperate amends those four needed to make. They were as bemused by the man as she was.

Katie kept her back firmly turned. She needed all her fragile defences, even the slight distance formality imposed. 'My Grandma Staunton was a bear for manners, Mr Reese. She'd make you a thimble pie if you forgot.' She turned and demonstrated the quick rap of knuckles against skull her grandmother had called a thimble pie. 'That's not a bad way to be.'

'True,' Jason agreed, neither amused nor rebuffed by her prickly refusal. She loved too hard, too completely to give even friendship lightly. 'Unfortunately, my grandmother was unable to impress her grandson with many manners. I prefer to call you Kathleen.'

'Whatever?' Katie shrugged, secretly pleased. She liked the sound of his voice saying Kathleen. It had the soft whisper of a lingering caress. Nobody called her Kathleen but him, that made it a little special.

'Before I forget——'

Katie eyed the twenty-dollar bill he was holding out with the same distaste she would have shown a dead rat. She hid her hands behind her back and her embarrassment behind lowered lashes. Just like a fool Northerner, she thought in angry splutters, apologising with one breath and insulting her hospitality with the next!

'No, sir,' she stammered. 'I was only being hateful when I said that,' she added to soothe her nagging conscience. After all, she had put the price tag on her hospitality.

'Kathleen, I insist.' Cool blue eyes flashed an imperious command.

That pride was one thing this young woman did not lack, was certain, that he had offended that pride was just as certain, but to refuse money which she did lack went beyond pride to obstinacy. Jason tried reason. 'This wouldn't even pay for a motel room.'

Stern Southern pride stiffened her spine and raised her eyes to challenge his. 'This isn't a motel, this is my home, and I do the insisting here. I won't take your money, but you're welcome to stay, for Poppet's sake,' she added so there would be no further misunderstandings.

She turned her head but watched him out of the corner of her eye. 'I think they're waiting for you, Mr Reese.'

She clamped her soft mouth into a firm line. She wasn't about to be laughed at, insulted, mocked or in any other way bamboozled by a fast-talking Yankee peddlerman. Even this one. Especially this one.

Jason pocketed the bill, bowing to her stubborn pride for the moment. As his grandmother had often said, there were more ways than one to skin a cat or tame a redheaded wildcat.

CHAPTER FOUR

'He's gone,' the rising morning wind whispered to the listening trees. 'Gone away. Gone away,' echoed the drowsy mourning doves.

Impatient with the conversation only her ears heard, Katie folded her pillow over her head. She kicked angrily at the sheet tangling her feet. Waking heavy-hearted to a house too quiet and empty because he was no longer in it and listening to birds and trees talk was pure foolishness.

Poppet stretched and wrinkled her nose, her sleep disturbed by Katie's thrashings. 'I've got a secret,' she announced with an enormous yawn.

'Going to tell me?' Katie asked.

'Nope!' Curling up on her side, her back to Katie, Poppet snuggled back into her comfortable cocoon of sleep.

Katie's frown melted into a smile. She kissed the tousled crown of blonde hair. Only a fool would call a house or a life filled with five children empty.

She slipped cautiously out of bed and turned off the alarm clock not scheduled to sound its irritating buzz for another twenty minutes. Common sense demanded that she use the gift of twenty free minutes for some practical purpose, but the hills sang their siren song and the newborn sun demanded her obeisance.

The cool dew bathed her bare feet and the sun warmed her shoulders through the thin fabric of her nightgown. The sheer joy of being alive filled her. She raised her arms to embrace the timbered ridges and the sun and the heavens. She wished she was an eagle soaring high and looking down on God's most perfect creation, her haze-shrouded hills. If she could not be an eagle, she would be Katie Claire Staunton and look up and never allow her eyes or her heart to grow tired of the beauty they saw.

She wished Jason was here—now. She would show him her wealth and explain that it was her duty to stop and look and enjoy her treasure so vast it was beyond counting, that to do anything less would be an unforgivable sin. She wanted to make him understand why so many generations of her family had hung on during bad times any way they could and why even those who had left cherished their heritage. She wanted him to see her heart, see her hills, see her.

'Um-m-m,' she hummed her exasperation and shook her head. It was a miracle that her stubborn one-track mind didn't hear the hills shout his name, so determined was it to turn every thought to him.

How could a computer understand and enjoy beauty? she asked in her mind with an impatient toss of her head. That was what he was, a computer, an uncaring and unfeeling machine. 'No, he isn't,' she admitted with a whispering sigh. She would not lie to herself. He was not a computer, he was very much a man—a strong man sure enough of his strength to be gentle. A man easy to fall in love with.

'And you're Katie Claire Staunton, not some dreaming fool of a girl,' she lectured herself sternly. 'You've got things to do and kids to raise, and you don't need anything else. Mr Jason Reese is a business proposition, pure and simple. That's the way it is and that's the way it's going to stay.'

Her chin jerked down in confident agreement. That was all her contrary heart needed, a little talking to. He was gone, and she was glad. Now things could get back to normal.

'Tail feathers!' Katie set her coffee down with a thump and glared at the cup as if it had somehow offended her. With the berries delivered, breakfast eaten, dishes done, the garden weeded, and a load of laundry contentedly sloshing, the brood split up and occupied out of hearing the quiet should have been as savoury as putting her feet up and enjoying a cup of coffee. Should have been, would have been, except for Joseph.

As usual Joseph had been waiting for them, waiting for her. The little ones distracted with sweet rolls, he had motioned her aside and asked how the weekend had gone.

Pretending to not know what he meant, Katie widened her eyes and shrugged, 'Fine.'

Folding his mouth into an angry pout, Joseph darted a glance at the children and sidled closer still to Katie. 'Girl, if you wiggle your tail feathers——' he paused to shake his hips—'right, you might just catch yourself a rich one.'

'And what's that supposed to mean?' asked Katie, knowing exactly what Joseph meant.

'Poppet's daddy,' he hissed.

'I haven't sunk that low!' she spat.

'Low!' Joseph howled in a whisper, glancing furtively at the brood. 'Girl, rich ain't no dirty word. Are you going to spend the rest of your life raising somebody else's babies? When you ought to be having your own and a man to go with them.'

'Joseph,' Katie warned, struggling to keep her temper. 'We're running late this morning. I'll see you Wednesday—that is, unless you'd rather buy your strawberries from somebody else.'

'Girl, you are pure stubborn, do you know that?' Joseph growled.

'I know,' Katie hissed, aiming a toothy leer and waggling her fingers at him and calling the little ones.

'Tail feathers!' Joseph shouted after her.

'Tail feathers,' Katie snorted. 'I never!' she insisted, glaring at the coffee cup.

The ringing telephone shattered the quiet that refused to be peaceful. Still muttering, 'Tail feathers,' she jerked the receiver from the cradle.

'Miss Kathleen Staunton?' a vaguely familiar masculine voice asked.

'Yes, this is me. This is she,' Katie grumbled.

'This is Burt Chillingham, down at the bank.'

She stared at the receiver. Burt Chillingham was Mr Chillingham, and he wasn't down at the bank, he was the bank.

'Mr Jason Reese had asked me to notify you of the direct deposit of funds to your account. He explained that direct transfer is more convenient for both of you and that the same sum is to be credited to your account the first of each month.'

Katie tilted her head and closed her eyes to make better sense out of what the babbling idiot on the other end of the line was saying. Her temper came to a slow simmer. Jason Reese had certainly handled that one very neatly. He had replaced the cheque she had torn up and found a way to prevent any future cheque-tearing incidents.

'How much did you say?' she hissed aloud.

When he repeated the amount her foot tapped a quick rhythm on the cool tile floor. That man! He'd tacked on the twenty dollars she'd refused. He wasn't one to take no for an answer. Well, she wasn't one to take what she didn't want.

'That's twenty dollars too much,' she insisted. 'You will send the twenty dollars back to Mr Reese.' When Burt Chillingham resisted her request with an indulgent chuckle her temper soared like the eagle she had earlier wanted to be. 'There are other banks,' she reminded him before slamming down the receiver.

She was still storming around the kitchen thoroughly enjoying her fit of righteous indignation when Jeeter crashed through the screen door, yelping at the top of his lungs for her to come. She scurried around the corner of the house with Jeeter and Poppet at her heels. It was Mr Kendall and his entire road-building crew.

'Katie.' He acknowledged her by sweeping off his straw hat and mopping his balding head with his shirt sleeve. 'Got orders here to grade and rock this here road of yours.'

'Oh!' Her widened eyes flared emerald green with anger. Her lane was private property. It was nobody else's concern and she hadn't ordered anything done to it.

'Yes, ma'am.' He nodded, agreeing with himself, and mopped his balding head again. Jamming his battered hat back on his head, he patted several pockets and muttered several words Katie couldn't quite make out. 'Right here it is, see.' He shoved a slip of paper at her. 'Right here. Paid for and all.' His work-grimed finger underlined the words scrawled diagonally across the work order. 'Charge to Mr Jason Reese. Must be done today,' he read for her, so she would know they both saw the same words.

'Is that right?' asked Katie, her normally soft voice dripping the bitter honey of sarcasm.

'Yes, ma'am.' Mr Kendall reddened and quailed under the lash of her rising fury.

'Well, Mr Kendall, I do the ordering around here.' Katie ripped the work order in two. 'And I do the paying.' She tore it again and presented him with the pieces.

He cleared his throat. 'Yes, ma'am.'

'Well, it does need doing,' she admitted. 'I do apologise for carrying on so, Mr Kendall.' She peeped up at him through the thick fringe of lashes shielding her eyes. 'Since you're here and it does need doing, I would like to have you repair my lane. If you'll come up to the house when you're finished, I'll give you a cheque.'

She raised her face, a flash of pride darkening her eyes. 'I trust you will inform Mr Reese that the work has been done and paid for and that his assistance is not required.'

'Sure enough, Miss Katie,' Mr Kendall nodded, tacking on the respectful miss to her name.

He continued bobbing his head at her retreating back. She didn't have that fire in her hair for nothing, that one. All temper and pride, like the old grandma had been in her day. It wasn't a bad way to be considering the way things were.

Mr Kendall scratched his ear thoughtfully. It was a funny ol' world. Some stranger important enough to set the boss on his ear wanted to pay for fixing Katie Staunton's lane and she was telling him to go to hell in no uncertain terms. That was one to tell the wife about!

Mr Kendall did seem to be doing a thorough job, Katie admitted, watching men and machines gouge and dump and smooth their way along the lane. That lane had been a disgrace for a good long while. He wasn't doing any work that the whole county didn't know needed doing.

The gall of that man! She dropped the curtain back in place and stormed across the room. The whole county might have known it, but at least they didn't have the low-down, plain-out, Northern brass to say so, let alone try to pay for it. Well, she'd certainly put the run to that little idea, Mr Jason Reese and his almighty cheque-book!

A wry smile touched her mouth, the truth was, either way he was paying for it. The only reason she could sign a cheque was because he had transferred the money. There is a difference, she reminded herself with a toss of her head. That was tax-deductible, income-reportable, earned money. The other would have been a gift, and gifts tended to have strings attached. She would not be beholden to that man. Theirs was a business arrangement and that was the way it was going to stay.

'And I'll be telling you that too,' she assured the discomfiting phantom of the man haunting her mind. 'I will,' she reiterated with a swift downward slash of her proud chin. 'Right now!'

She swept through the house, unconsciously delighted to have found the legitimate target for the restlessness that had lashed out at Mr Kendall. Telephone numbers, home and office, had been provided to be used in case of an emergency. This was not the kind of emergency Sister Claire had envisaged, but it was close enough to suit Katie.

She allowed her temper to rise to a roiling boil as she dialled the string of numbers and mentally rehearsed the tirade she would deliver. She was going to singe his ears but good! Barefoot little hillbilly, was she? Too ignorant to know better, was she? She'd teach him a thing or two!

A crisp, uninterested female voice answered by announcing the telephone number she had dialled.

'Mr Jason Reese, please,' Katie requested, her bubbling tantrum brought down to a tepid whisper by cool reality.

'I'm sorry, Mr Reese is on another line, may I take a message?'

'I'll hold,' insisted Katie, regaining some of her self-assurance.

'Who is calling, please?' Jen Marshall knew all the voices privy to Mr Reese's unlisted number. But not this one—young, female and with an accent thick enough to cut with a knife. Jen was too good a secretary to broadcast her boss's business, but the grapevine was already buzzing with his highly unusual and unexplained absence on Friday. Jen was a good secretary but also very human. She also typed some of Mr Reese's cheques for his personal account and relayed personnel reports.

'Kathleen Staunton,' Katie answered with as much professional briskness as her drawl would allow. 'It's not an emergency,' she added, not wanting to unnecessarily alarm him.

'Kathleen?'

'Yes, sir,' Katie snapped, steeling herself against the image of him that rose unbidden to tickle her pulses when Jason answered, after what seemed eons but was no more than three minutes.

'We have a non-emergency?'

'I pay my own bills, Mr Reese,' Katie spluttered, retreating behind a wall of temper, her best defence against the overpowering masculinity four hundred miles blunted but did not entirely defeat. 'That is my lane, and it will be my lane when you're long gone and forgotten. I wanted it rocked. I paid for it.'

'Kathleen,' Jason soothed. He'd been expecting this call. 'It was meant as a token of my appreciation, a gift for a gracious hostess.'

The image of him, his chair tilted back, his long powerful legs casually crossed, his head thrown back and tilted to one side, the quirking half smile that accompanied the dancing laughter in his eyes, knotted her stomach. She silently cursed him and her over-active imagination.

'Hostess gift, my foot!' she raged. He was laughing at her, mocking her again. 'A hostess gift is a box of chocolates or a dozen roses or a bottle of wine. Not a road!' She glared at the telephone and the man it connected her to.

'I see.'

His reasonable calm served only to goad her to new heights. 'And I sent back your twenty dollars too!' she snapped.

'Twenty dollars,' Jason wondered aloud, as if it was such a small matter he had forgotten it. That too had been expected and perhaps was more successful than

the road, since she was furious enough over the twenty
dollars to forget that she was keeping the rest. 'Yes, of
course, that twenty dollars. Is there anything else?'

'No, sir,'Katie managed to answer in a tone that was
a fair imitation of his maddening patience.

'Very well. Have a good day, Kathleen.'

She slammed down the receiver before he could
hang up on her. That man! She hurled the telephone
book at the refrigerator. Her actions did nothing to
soothe the storm of her emotions.

Looking as pleased as Katie had imagined, Jason
chuckled softly. His wildcat wasn't quite tame—yet. He
doubted if she ever would be.

'Sure is hot, Katie.' Jeeter mopped his forehead and
blew out a long breath.

'That right?' teased Katie, knowing full well what
the boy had in mind. It was Friday and a scorcher of
a day.

The vision of the cool, clear creek with its golden
sand bed and overhanging canopy of whispering leaves
danced through her head. How refreshing it would be
to plunge into the spring-fed coolness and stretch out
on a sunwarmed blanket for an hour or so. Her eyes
clouded as she hardened her heart and mouth to such
foolishness. That had been one of his complaints, her
willingness to postpone what should be done in favour
of clearing dancing floors or exploring attics or going
swimming.

She raised her chin, her narrowed eyes darkening
with anger. What did he know? Dirty clothes would
wait patiently for her to return; little ones would not
wait to grow up.

'If you're too busy to take them, big sister, I'll do it.'
Chance ducked low enough to fit himself and his
shoulder-riding passenger, Poppet, through the door.

Katie grinned up at him. Chance at not quite sixteen

had at last matched and surpassed her height and was rather proud of it.

'The day I'm too busy to go swimming, little brother, is the day I'll be dead.' She paused, nibbling her full underlip. It was possible to both work and play. 'You little ones, mind Chance,' she ordered. 'Go on ahead and I'll catch up.'

After issuing appropriate warnings several times, Katie watched after them until the twisting path shut them from her view. She ran upstairs to change into her swimsuit and then to the pantry to stuff the washing machine. It was a compromise worthy of a statesman, she told herself. While she was swimming, the laundry would be started and allowed to complete its allotted cycle, simultaneously serving both practicality and pleasure. Jason Reese and his computers couldn't have planned better.

'Oh, fiddle!' Katie muttered when the telephone rang before she could escape the broad back porch and safely ignore its summons.

A shiver of excitement skittered down her spine when she recognised the low-pitched voice speaking her name.

'Yes, sir,' she answered, seeking something to cover the clinging gold one-piece swimsuit hugging her body. The fact that Jason was several hundred miles away and blind to whatever she might be wearing was completely irrelevant. 'Poppet went swimming, but I can call her back for you,' she stammered as she wound a beach towel over her suit.

'No, I can call back later. I promised to bring her something this weekend if I could get away, but I'm afraid I'm going to be tied up here. I have a lot of homework to do.'

Glaring at the concealing towel that concealed nothing that needed concealing, Katie tore it loose and pitched it at the table. She ignored the tinge of exhaustion in his voice and pounced instead on what she concluded was a broken promise, Poppet's secret.

'Well, if it's homework, Mr Reese, why don't you just bring it on home?' she snapped.

'I can imagine how much I would accomplish with five children in a house ten miles from nowhere,' answered Jason, replacing ineffectual exhaustion with sarcasm.

'You're forgetting, sir, that I work at home, and my father did too. They know that when the study door is closed they're to take their noise elsewhere. And it's not ten miles, it's seven miles. We have a telephone and a four-wheel-drive vehicle capable of going anywhere. I do believe the world can totter along without you for a weekend,' Katie spat back, rising to his bait and thoroughly enjoying herself.

'Very well, since you insist. You can pick me up at— er—around seven at the Windjammer.'

'What?' wailed Katie. She hadn't expected him to agree with her lunatic idea, let alone order her to fetch him.

'Unless you've cleared a very large dancing floor, the nearest landing strip is at Tara,' Jason explained patiently.

'Yes, sir. Of course,' Katie agreed, hoping she had concealed her surprise and thankful he wasn't able to see her staring at the telephone with her mouth hanging open.

She shook her head in an attempt to free herself of the lingering effects of that most unusual conversation and wondered whatever had come over her. Not that it made any difference, she realised, what was done was done. He was coming, she was fetching, and the little ones had to be told.

For the first time in recorded history Jeeter and Poppet didn't have to be ordered out of the water. Her announcement filled their minds with so many important and secret plans that in less than an hour even their feet were jiggling. With a regretful glance over her shoulder at the older three still splashing in the inviting coolness, Katie followed the scheming pair back to the house.

Once in the house Katie was gradually enlightened. First Poppet shyly suggested eating supper in the dining room, after her father arrived. When Katie agreed, Jeeter pointed out that the walnut harvest table, on such a grand occasion, deserved the best table linens. The linen in turn deserved the silver candlesticks, which they volunteered to polish. The polished candlesticks looked very lonesome on such a big table by themselves. They needed the company of the silver bowl, which they had also polished, just in case Katie wanted flowers.

Katie allowed herself to be charmed into following their lead, telling herself that it wouldn't hurt for Jason to see her brood in a more civilised setting. She sacrificed the best of her red roses and directed their attention to the choicest ferns on the far side of the spring house. She laid a moderating hand on their high-flown dreams of hors d'oeuvres and a fountain of champagne on the dancing floor, followed by a combination of every exotic-sounding food they had ever heard of. They struck a compromise, settling for an enormous tossed salad with all the trimmings and spaghetti, which Katie explained would not dry out or fall flat if they were delayed. She also promised a thimbleful of wine all around, if Mr Reese did not object.

After sniffing all the good smells emanating from the kitchen and taking an ever so casual stroll through the dining room with its sparkling array of crystal and silver and Great-Granny's china, the older three realised that this was a matter of honour and thundered upstairs to primp.

By six they were assembled in a fidgeting row in the living room, watching the clock and trying to maintain an aura of sophisticated nonchalance without wrinkling or mussing anything. Katie took pity on them and declared she must show them off. Carefully concealing the double-crossed fingers of her left hand, she remembered reading that some nationality or other always ate dessert before their meal. She proposed treating her beautiful young lady and handsome men to dessert in the main dining room at Tara.

They trooped in an orderly procession out to the truck and settled into their assigned places without so much as one elbow in the ribs. There was something in the tilt of Katie's chin that warned, one mis-step and she would high-step them from truck to kitchen using any handy ear she could locate for a leash.

Wagging his head and grinning, Joseph circled the table, pausing to look each one over carefully, lest his eyes be playing tricks on him.

'My daddy's coming home!' Poppet's joy bubbled over into giggles.

'Is he now?' Joseph hunkered down beside her chair.

Poppet nodded and launched into a detailed description of their afternoon activities.

'That Katie is bringing you up right. A man deserves a royal welcome after working all week.' Joseph leered knowingly at Katie and added a wink of approval.

'Weren't Katie's idea,' Jeeter piped. 'Me and Poppet, we thought up the whole thing, all by ourselves.'

'Somehow I don't doubt that for one minute.' Joseph's knowing grin faded into an exasperated frown. He straightened up and hovered over Katie. 'But then the Good Book does say that a little child shall lead them, and I never in all my born days ever saw a grown woman in such need of leading.'

Katie sipped her coffee and ignored his criticism. She told herself that her face was warm because the dining room was inexcusably overheated. It was on the tip of her tongue to ask if the air-conditioning was broken.

Gripping her shoulders with just enough pressure to be sure of her attention, her godfather brought his mouth close to her ear. 'You ever hear of an invention called a skirt, girl?'

Katie clamped her mouth into a firm line and twisted her head to challenge his impertinent gaze. Her first impulse had been just that, to wear the dress she had bought for no good reason a few days earlier. Yellow gauze print with deep crocheted lace inserts, it was softly feminine and totally seductive, exploiting the golden tone of her flawless skin and reflecting and intensifying the hidden flecks of amber in her eyes. Instead, practising contrary logic, she had chosen wheat-coloured slacks and an equally neutral blouse. She left her costume sternly unornamented, even stripping off the tiny gold stud earrings she habitually wore, and imprisoned her wealth of hair in a no-nonsense knot on the nape of her slender neck. No flirting.

'Skirts are draughty,' she hissed.

Joseph groaned under his breath and rapped the top of her head with his knuckles before ambling off in search of other, more malleable guests.

After an endless ten minutes one of the bartenders, an acquaintance from her drink-serving days, appeared in the doorway. Katie nodded and smiled her thanks and with a quick downward slash of her hand, invisible to the other diners, ordered the brood to remain seated. The dimly lit Windjammer, the more intimate of Tara's two lounges, didn't admit that anyone under the legal drinking age of twenty-one existed.

She aimed another smile at the bartender when he pointed at Jason seated at a secluded corner table, this one tight and toothy. One more ounce of curiosity and it would have come bubbling out of the man's ears.

She politely refused Jason's offer to join him and
remained censoriously upright while he finished his
drink. The bartender didn't possess the only pair of
flapping ears and Katie didn't care to be the subject of
any more juicy titbits of gossip. Half the county had
seen or heard about him sitting in the front seat of her
truck, sitting very close, closer with every telling. And
those who hadn't seen had heard about the lane.

'The little ones are waiting,' she explained, her chin
angled so haughtily she had to almost close her eyes to
see down to where he was sitting. Surely it was her
impaired vision or a trick of the flickering candle and
not regret that briefly shadowed his rough-hewn face.
'They worked all evening on a surprise for you,' she
added more sharply than she intended.

'Evening?' A raised eyebrow questioned her use of
the term while the sun was still up.

'You're in Missouri, Mr Reese; around here our
evenings start at two o'clock. You'd best leave your
Northern notions of time up north,' she snapped.

'It would seem that I would be well advised to leave a
good many Northern notions up north,' he answered
drily.

'It would seem best,' Katie agreed, leading the way
through the maze of tables that she had once threaded
as a waitress.

There was a brief tussle over the dining room check
when Jason insisted on paying by virtue of his rights as
a man and the natural payer of restaurant check.
Katie countered, unsuccessfully, with the fact that she
had done the ordering and that she would do the
paying. Amusement curved his chiselled mouth into an
enticingly mischievous grin and twinkled in his deep-set
eyes, reminding her that he had heard those words
before but did nothing to loosen his hold on the bill.
Katie slapped down a tip guaranteed to open the eyes
of the most jaded waitress and shooed the brood out

ahead of her, being extra careful to not shake the tail
feathers Joseph had recommended she shake at the man
behind her.

Their dinner party was a brilliant success. Jason's
compliments on their efforts were numerous and
admiring, but stopped short of the extravagance adults
sometimes indulged in when dealing with children.
Katie's stiff formality stood out in stark contrast and
puzzled the brood. They sought to relieve her
discomfort by relating her various and sundry accom-
plishments. When she objected by word or action they
paid her no mind; manners dictated that the one being
praised deny any need of praise, and Katie was a bear
for manners.

She did not give in to her earnest desire and bang
their heads together. Instead she was quietly and
politely furious, boiling mad at them for rattling on
about bits of nonsense long gone and best forgotten,
furious with Jason for hearing out their tales of her
triumphs with the same grave courtesy he had shown
them and thoroughly aggravated with herself for caring
what he thought.

She put her fury to good use by tackling the dishes
while they helped him settle his temporary office in the
study. When he strolled in and helped himself to a dish-
towel, her hard-kept reserve snapped. She was brief but
left no doubts. She wasn't about to have a man
mooching around in her kitchen, putting things away in
all the wrong places, making more work than he was
saving. If he thought she was any less efficient or
organised in her work than he was in his, she advised
him to think again.

He did not turn tail and run as she hoped. Rather, he
gravely considered her words, the tilt of her chin and
the anger blazing in her eyes and agreed, leaving her to
her work.

Not even balling up the towel and pitching it at the

refrigerator helped. Jason Reese was positively the most
infuriating man there ever had been, Katie assured
herself. Besides, she admitted with a shrug as she
retrieved the towel, it would have been impossible to
maintain the necessary ten feet if he had dried the
dishes while she washed them. Not that the ten feet was
necessary any longer. The only emotion he elicited was
intense loathing. He had a calculator for a heart and a
cheque book for a conscience. He was totally bereft of
moral values, an egotistical, conceited, ill-mannered,
hedonistic fool, and he treated her like a child—and a
none too bright one at that!

By the time the kitchen was straightened, Katie was
thoroughly enjoying her fit of righteous indignation and
almost convinced of its validity.

'Come on. Come on, Katie!' Poppet and Jeeter
insisted in unison, each tugging at a hand.

She hummed a questioning, 'Ummm?' and scowled
with mock severity and allowed them to lead her out to
the dancing floor. Whatever they were up to had them
nearly bursting with excitement.

'This one's for you.' Poppet presented Katie with a
beautifully wrapped rectangle and waited, eyes glowing,
for her to open it.

'Jay brought every one of us something.' Jeeter
nodded and wiggled, encouraging Katie to open hers
and free them to tear into theirs.

'Why, thank you.' Katie brushed Poppet's cheek with a
kiss. 'And thank you too, Mr Reese.' She raised her head
proudly and favoured Jason with a barely civil nod.

The boys followed with a chorus of yelped 'thank
you's' and dived for their own packages. Katie bit the
inside of her lip and stared proudly past him. The entire
episode smacked of charity, and she could not easily
thank him for that.

Pride and something she could not name struggled
for ascendancy. He had chosen his gifts well—a box of

chocolates for her, the perfect and personally recommended hostess gift, one she could not refuse. Chance was already demonstrating the Ultra-Lite rod and reel he had been craving. Bo and Rocky had received books and supplies that set their hands to itching and their minds to thinking about new and better lab experiments. Jeeter whooped and pounded the pocket of the fielder's mitt he had admired for so long and Katie hadn't been able to buy for him.

Jason had sorted out the brood faster than anyone ever had, matching name to face and spirit. Katie thanked him again but avoided meeting his eyes.

Poppet bounced out of bed and insisted on telling her father the tale of the Louisiana Bride and her bed one more time. Growling a completely non-threatening warning in her throat, Katie captured the small body in her arms and held her close. Poppet had requested that both Jason and Katie accompany her to bed, but any thought of going to sleep had been long since forgotten.

'Your eyes are sealed and nothing but the morning sun can open them,' Katie intoned as she touched the little one's eyelids. Her eyes closed, Poppet collapsed in Katie's arms, as boneless as a rag doll. The unscientific art of eye-glueing had worked again as Katie had known it would. It had worked on her too. She had been a big girl of four or five before she realised that her mother couldn't actually glue her eyes shut, and the spell, even debunked, had kept its potency for some years after.

'Ah, Katie,' Poppet pleaded, with absolutely no hope of reprieve.

'No, now I mean it. Morning comes early and I can't do without my official counter.' Katie cast a longing glance at the bed some feet away. Poppet relaxed and feigning sleep was much heavier than Poppet bouncing and clinging.

Wordlessly, Jason took the little girl into his own strong arms and carried her to bed.

'Kiss, Daddy,' Poppet insisted, puckering up, her eyes scrunched tightly closed by the magic glue Katie had applied.

Jason chuckled, the warm throaty sound of a man pleased with life, and bent his dark head over her fair one. 'Now I know how to put you to sleep,' he teased gently.

'Katie knows everything,' Poppet bragged. She wrapped her arms around his neck. 'You'll be here in the morning?'

'I'll be here,' he whispered huskily, rocking her in the cradle of his arms.

Katie averted her eyes, feeling the intruder in her own bedroom. Whatever else she might be able to convince herself he was, Jason loved his daughter.

'Kathleen.'

Katie flinched from the electrification of her senses that was his fingers brushing her arm. She bobbed her head, understanding. He had played the gentleman all evening, but he hadn't been as pleased as he had led the children to believe. Now the computer was going to present its print out of complaints. Head high, spine stiff, Katie led the way to the kitchen. If they were to skirmish again it would be in the very heart of her domain.

Jason leaned his potently masculine frame against the counter, his long legs casually crossed, his head thrown back, and watched her with a disturbing intensity.

Katie retreated to a safer distance, the other side of the room, and assumed a casual stance, leaning against the refrigerator with her arms crossed under her breasts, her hands hidden under her elbows in case she had reason to double-cross her fingers. She commanded her quivering heart to remember that he was not a man, he was Poppet's father, and that this was business. She sternly told herself that she did not want to be crushed to his hard chest, she did not want to feel the intimate caress of his lips kissing her goodnight.

She glared at him and struck with her only effective weapon, anger. 'How could you leave your child with strangers? People you didn't even know? Just leave her without a thought?'

'At your request,' he answered calmly, with a hint of a smile as if he had been expecting her attack.

'No such thing!' Katie retorted, joining battle joyfully.

'No?' Amusement tugged at the corner of his mouth and danced impishly in his eyes. 'That's funny, I was under the impression that you wanted two months with Alicia without any disruption such as a father. I must have misunderstood Sister Claire. Just as you misunderstood.'

'What are you talking about?' she demanded, her eyes flashing an angry denial.

'Shall we say that the angels are often glad that my aunt is on their side.'

'Are you suggesting that Sister Claire, a nun, lied?' Katie huffed, knowing and not caring that she was adding her thoughts to his statement.

'Yes.' There was a definite undertow of amusement in his voice. 'But as she pointed out when I confronted her, only the once. The rest of the time she and Alicia simply allowed us to jump to our own wrong conclusions. And we did, in spades. You aren't a middle-aged widow and I'm not a child-deserting monster. But the most important thing is that Alicia is happy here—happy enough to be a kid instead of a miniature adult. We were both wrong, Kathleen, so why don't we just start over?'

Katie ducked his enticing lopsided grin encouraging her to agree. She wanted to agree with anything and everything he said, to please him, to have his eyes linger and soften as they became aware of the woman she was.

Jerking her chin up, Katie pulled her mouth into a firm line to ward off such traitorous thoughts.

'Will there be anything else, sir?' she enquired stiffly.

'Yes,' drawled Jason, watching her with half-closed eyes that were distinctly unsleepy. She wasn't going to evade him that easily.

Poised for flight, Katie took a half step before realising that he had not released her. Very well, her pursed lips and narrowed eyes said as her frustrated temper exulted. There wasn't a man made that Katie Claire Staunton couldn't face down.

'You object to my gifts?'

'Yes, sir,' she snapped.

'Why?' The dark wings of his brows gathered thoughtfully.

'Gifts have strings,' she insisted with a proud toss of her head. 'Strings,' she reiterated through the pain threatening to crush her heart. 'Strings on them. You'll make a place for yourself in their hearts and then you'll walk away. They have enough holes in their hearts already, they don't need any more.'

'And you, Kathleen,' Jason probed gently. 'You give so freely, but you're so afraid to take. Is that what you're afraid of, that someone will put strings on you and tie you down and then walk away?'

'I take care of me and mine. We don't need anybody else,' Katie insisted, her chin assuming its familiar upward thrust, daring him to challenge her. 'Now, if you'll excuse me, Mr Reese, morning does come early and I do have strawberries to peddle,' she added with a certain malicious delight in being able to remind herself as well as him that he wasn't a necessary part of her life, that she was doing just fine without him.

CHAPTER FIVE

KATIE raised her eyes to the hills, resplendent in their summer finery, answering the call only her ears heard. Smiling, she promised to join them when the sun hid behind his purple and rose mantle of clouds and the evening wind told the trees what had been and what would be.

Only the hills knew that June had been a golden haze slipping through her fingers, a blur of days haunted by Jason—a haunting she kept well hidden from all but the ancient ones. They knew how eagerly she awaited Friday and his coming and dreaded Sunday sundown and his leaving. They understood the restless longings that had grown into an agonising ache. They knew that her chilly formality and determined avoidance of Jason was a brittle façade and her prickly anger a thin veneer, her only defences against the swirling cross-currents he created in her life.

Only the hills knew her heart, and they guarded their child's secret as closely as she did. She felt their strength reaching out to her in the gentle caress of the breeze commanding her to feel, hear and taste the perfection of now, to enjoy the wealth of the day.

Reassured by the hills that knew centuries as nothing more than fleeting shadows, Katie stepped back into the kitchen still fragrant with the aroma of strawberry jam freshly sealed and cooling on the counter. Allowing herself a moment of gloating pride, she gazed at the jewel-like clarity of the jam, part of the wealth the hills had reminded her to cherish. More precious than rubies, it was not only a treat for the eye, it was a treat for the palate as well.

She savoured the sweet satisfaction of knowing that she was providing for her family against the barren winter to come. Silent laughter curved her generous mouth and danced in her eyes, mocking such high-flown fancies. The Staunton farm was no longer self-sufficient; if they had to rely on her relatively small store of canned and frozen goods they would be hungry to starvation long before spring. But the joy the hills had commanded prevailed; she was Katie Claire Staunton, with wealth beyond counting.

The noise of a car nosing its way along the well-gravelled length of the lane pulled her to the front of the house and gathered her full underlip in a pout. She didn't want to share her new-found joy with outsiders, especially not with Miss Hawk, the social worker, whose long nose was leading her to the house.

Katie groaned. Trust efficient Miss Hawk—her usual visitation day was the first Wednesday of the month, which would fall on the Fourth of July this coming month, Independence Day, a holiday. Trust efficient Miss Hawk to come a week early, not a day late! Katie shrugged her shoulders, accepting what she could not change. The woman was here.

On the first Wednesday of the month for almost five years Miss Hawk had sat in Katie's parlour and laid down new rules and made new demands. Their first skirmishes had ended in a courtroom with Miss Hawk arguing that Tommie and Marie Staunton's wills were unfair and should be set aside. She called Katie a mere child herself and said that the guardianship of her brothers was a legal afterthought which would become a fourteen-year prison sentence, not the safeguard her parents had intended. Through her lawyer, Katie argued that under federal law she was a voting age adult, that she could contract business or marry without the consent of parent or guardian. She was not a child and intent could not be ascertained, that the court had no choice but to abide by the content of those contested wills.

Katie won that round, and the next a few months later when Miss Hawk, claiming concern for the minor children, the boys, requested an accounting and some kind of guarantee that the equitable distribution of property, which had been left entirely to Katie's discretion, would be equitable. Again the judge ruled that the wills stood, but he suggested that because of Katie's tender years she avail herself of the services and professional expertise of the Department of Social Services.

Katie took great care to never avail herself of anything Miss Hawk had to offer. Always she managed to stay one jump ahead of the woman. She would this time too.

They exchanged wary pleasantries and took their places in opposing chairs.

A dozen years had stripped Nancy Hawk of any illusions she might have had about social work and social workers. She no longer believed she could single-handedly make the world a better place or even make much of an impact on it, but she kept trying. She recognised that the bureaucracy she was a part of was a lumbering, sick giant that sometimes crushed those it was commissioned to aid. She knew her clients lied to her, not necessarily maliciously. Foxing the social worker was almost a point of honour. Most were simply proud people forced by circumstances they could not control to trade pride for survival. They resented being forced into such a position. They resented her, some quietly, some not so quietly, but none more than Katie Staunton.

She knew from experience that the girl was so busy planning her needless defence she would hear only a tenth of what was said, and only the Good Lord knew how she would rearrange that ten per cent. Once she had tried to explain to the girl that she was eligible for a four-hundred-dollar fuel grant—a grant, not a loan, it did not have to be repaid. Katie had responded by selling eighteenth-century pewter and presenting a copy of her paid fuel bill. The girl simply refused to understand that villains no longer existed, so she had created one and named it Nancy Hawk.

It took some time for Katie to follow the winding route Miss Hawk was taking, but then the woman never did rush in headlong. What she wanted was always well camouflaged under a deluge of words.

Katie's spine stiffened. Miss Hawk chattered on, congratulating her on providing so well for the little ones' physical needs. The woman's thin mouth stretched into a smile. She wondered aloud, with another spate of words, about damaged psyche. She sighed mournfully for three boys struggling towards manhood with no father figure to lead them. She strengthened her position with 'role pattern', 'adolescent trauma' and 'budding male sexuality'.

Katie kept her face a perfect mask of rapt attention, feigning absolute interest in the pearls of wisdom rolling off Miss Hawk's silver-plated tongue. As she listened her mind raced back and forth, picking out key words and rearranging them. Translated into plain English the woman meant: You're not married and have no prospects—I've checked. You're too young and not married and therefore unfit to raise three impressionable young boys. (Rocky, of course, remained officially uncounted.) Just try and wriggle out of this one, another of those thin smiles added.

Nancy Hawk folded her hands and waited. She thought she had handled that very well. There was no way the girl could interpret that other than the way it was intended, that she knew about Jason Reese being here and considered him good for the boys.

Neither words nor actions betrayed Katie's absolute

terror. She nodded pleasantly. The pinch-faced woman had found a new demand. She wanted a bona fide man in their lives, a husband for Katie and a role pattern for the boys. There was nothing to do but go and get one.

'I'm getting married later this summer,' she announced.

She saw the glitter in Miss Hawk's eyes and crossed the fingers of her left hand. She'd already told one whopper of a lie, a slight untruth wouldn't do any more harm. 'Now, if you'll excuse me, you caught me right in the middle of a double batch of jam.'

She led the stunned social worker out of the house and down the porch steps to her car before she could ask any questions Katie couldn't answer, such as 'who'. With a cheery wave Katie sent her on her way.

Then she slipped into the quiet study and hid, shivering, in her father's chair. All the life-giving warmth of the June day had fled. Burying her face in her hands, she wondered how long she could fox the ferret-nosed social worker this time. 'Not long enough,' she moaned, answering her own worst fears.

Shaking her head, she raised her eyes to the hills and begged them to help her. A slanting ray of sunlight led her eyes to the statue of St Jude her mother had given her father, with the teasing comment that they should get along quite well since both were so fond of impossible causes.

'Help me,' she begged, 'and I'll do something for You.' It was wrong to try to bargain with God or His saints, she knew, but she didn't care. Right now she'd strike a bargain with the devil himself, if he made a good enough offer.

'Katie!' It was Jeeter searching the house for her.

'I'm in the study,' Katie called as she rearranged her face and shoved the problem of Miss Hawk to the back of her mind.

'Ol' Hawkface gone?' He grinned at her from the doorway.

'The lady's name is Miss Hawk,' Katie corrected. Jeeter was old enough to know that no one could tell him what to think, but thinking wasn't necessarily saying.

'Did she notice the lane?'

Katie hardened her mouth against a smile. He was getting wily.

'She didn't say, but then I don't see how she could have missed it.'

'Did you tell her that we got a new water heater?'

'No, I forgot.' Katie snapped her fingers at another of the improvements Jason's funds had helped into being. 'But then she didn't know we needed one, so it was most likely best I didn't tell her we got one.' She grinned at Jeeter and winked, a silent signal that no outsider had ever got the best of a Staunton yet and Miss Hawk wasn't about to start leading the parade.

Jeeter gnawed his underlip and studied Katie hard, not at all convinced that she was feeling as cheerful as she was acting.

'What did she say?' His fear balled his hands into fists and pushed them into his thighs.

'Nothing much.' Katie shrugged with elaborate casualness. 'Just how happy she was to see us getting along so well and how much you all had grown.'

Jeeter snorted his disbelief. He was as certain as Katie was that Miss Hawk had been put on this earth for no other reason than to harass the Stauntons. 'I wish that old bat would fall in the lake and never come up.'

'John Carter Staunton!' warned Katie, the use of his full name reassuring the boy that this particularly loathsome outsider was no closer to getting ahead of Katie than she ever had been.

'Yes, ma'am.' He hung his head to demonstrate his proper shame, then he peeped up at her, genuine devilment sparkling his blue eyes. 'It's getting powerful hot, Katie.'

'Usually does this time of day,' Katie allowed, knowing full well what he was up to. 'Do you suppose I could talk you boys into toting hot dogs and marshmallows down to the creek for a cook-out?'

'Just might be you could do that.' His tone was thoughtful, but he was wriggling like a happy puppy.

'Go and see what the others say,' Katie ordered.

Besides, she thought as she listened to him thunder down the hall, reassured that all was right with his world and eager to tell the others, Miss Hawk wouldn't risk her high heels on the twisting path that led to the creek if she gathered her wits together enough to return and ask 'who' and 'when'.

Unhearing, unfeeling, insensitive to the surrounding hills and to the too quiet children, Katie hatched and discarded schemes. It wasn't as if finding a husband was a new idea. She had always hoped to find a love as deep and abiding as the love her parents had shared, a love like the sun, warming all it touched.

Jason? The thought was dismissed before it could be formed.

She balled her hands into fists; she was a fool, dreaming of love, waiting for something that might never come. She had one loyalty, her family, and one duty, keeping them together. Nothing else mattered.

A bitter smile touched her lips. Miss Hawk's other demands had been comparatively easy to meet, requiring only sufficient money. Easy? Had it been easy to sell off bits and pieces of her heritage? Would her grandchildren understand that the eighteenth-century pewter the original Eli Staunton had brought along when he followed Mr Boone to Missouri was nice but fuel in the middle of winter was nicer? That first winter had been hell. If that was hell, then what was this to lose now when she no longer had to squeeze every penny until it did a nickel's worth of work?

Hysterical laughter bubbled in her throat, dangerously close to her lips. It was unfortunate one could not purchase a husband. Thanks to Jason her bank account was plump enough to afford a good, used economy model. A used husband lot? Why not? Why not a lease-a-man agency? Why buy if she could rent?

She did laugh, a full-bodied yelp of laughter, and tossed double handsful of sand in the air. There was such a thing. There were want ads for husbands, only they were called personal ads. Almost every major Sunday paper had a good supply of them.

'It's a day for living,' she called to the slumbering hills. 'And the living require food,' she informed the goggle-eyed brood.

Swirling waves of thought assaulted her brain. She didn't need a husband, not the genuine article. All she needed was the outward semblance of a marriage, a warm body to trot out for Miss Hawk's monthly examination. What she needed was a lease, a business proposition, an old-fashioned swap; free board and room in a restful country retreat in exchange for the use of a last name.

She couldn't be that blunt, of course. Yes, she could be. Personal ads were blunt if nothing else. But she wouldn't use her name; she'd die of mortification if anybody ever found out. She'd rent a post office box, not in Camdenton either, one of the other towns ringing the lake. That would keep Miss Hawk off the scent, and the brood too.

She couldn't invite just anybody down to marry her. She would require references and check them out too. He would have to like children, that went without saying, and be sober and goodnatured and like the quiet—and—and Prince Charming riding up on a white charger would do just dandy. Or Jason.

Frowning at her stubborn one-track mind, Katie again pushed away that enticing thought. She thumped the side of her head with the heel of her hand. It would take a bit of thinking to settle all the details in her mind and the brood, reacting to her change in mood, was already clamouring for her attention.

The appearance of Katie and her handsome covy of children caused barely a ripple in the surface murmur of Tara's main dining room. To those who did not know them they were simply an attractive group of well-mannered children. Those who knew better did their whispering in more private places.

Katie, aware of the buzz of gossip surrounding her week-end boarder, accepted it as part of living in a small close-knit community and ignored it. Since no one was brazen enough to ask for details, she volunteered none. Those who chose to believe the worst would not be dissuaded and those whom she valued were too tactful to ask, excluding the still hopeful Joseph. However, Katie was aware of the general consensus, that if she had a brain in her head she would tie him up but fast, by fair means or foul.

She smiled ruefully at her cup of coffee. What would those wagging tongues say when a second man showed up on manless Katie Staunton's doorstep? It would be enough to keep them clattering throughout the winter.

Her smile waned and the fear that had clouded her face for two days and haunted her dreams returned. Driven by that fear, she had set her plan in motion. The post office box was rented and the copy for her ad, edited to the necessary less than twenty words, was hidden in her handbag. She would mail it Monday, she promised herself, hoping that by then desperation would give her the necessary nerve. Allowing for three appearances in the Sunday *Post-Dispatch*, three additional weeks to consider and screen applicants, and two weeks to make her final decision, she would be safely married long before first frost painted her hills.

Her mind twisted and turned and fed on its own

fears. She questioned her ability to do anything in absolute secrecy. The brood had already noticed her preoccupation. She exulted in her discovery of a Sunday supplement story on mail-order marriages that worked, and brooded over the fact that most mass murderers were usually described as the nice-boy-next-door type with excellent references.

She shook her head and smiled absently at the brood in an attempt to dispel the worries that sharpened the planes of her face and shadowed her eyes. There was nothing to worry about; it would all be very civilised and temporary. There was no other way.

A flurry of activity roused her worried mind. She looked up and quickly jerked her eyes from the man searching the room for them. Jason had arrived, his presence electrifying the air with a charge that sent more than her bemused senses reeling. Already, a waitress was fluttering around the table in anticipation.

'I suppose this had already been paid for!' Jason asked, accepting the waitress's offer of coffee with a wry grin that made her an eager conspirator in a private joke, Katie's refusal to allow him to pay for her treat.

''Fraid so,' the woman quipped. A raised brow and coy smile added that she wouldn't be so foolish as to refuse his favours—any favours.

Katie suffered a stab of jealousy as he refused the unspoken offer with an appreciative smile that acknowledged everything he was refusing. She hid behind her coffee cup and sternly reminded herself that his private life was not her concern. She was paid to look after his child, nothing more. He was under no vow of celibacy, and just because he had the good manners not to tote one along when he came to see that child it didn't mean that he didn't have a mistress tucked away somewhere.

Her heart squeezed painfully as she pictured Jason making love to another woman, murmuring love names, his lips seeking and finding the sensitive hollow of her throat, the valley of her breasts, his hands exploring and caressing his faceless lady.

She bit her lip and concentrated on the glass wall to her left and the lake beyond. Theirs was a business arrangement, she reminded herself; she'd be well advised to remember that and keep on remembering that, if she had any sense. Miss Hawk had presented her with sufficient problems; she didn't need to invite more by daydreaming about Jason Reese.

Again her mind edged up to the idea of Jason as husband, then skittered to a far corner and hid. That was not even to be considered. She had never gained any immunity to his potent masculinity. If anything her fascination had grown. The way he held his head, the width of his shoulders, the power of his supple body, the sound of his voice welling up out of his chest, these were all indelibly etched in her mind. The quick glimpse she had allowed herself had been enough for her hungry mind to fill itself with every detail of his longed-for presence. It had noted the details of his clothing, the rich brown of his slacks moulded to his powerful thighs, the silkiness of the cream-coloured shirt sliding smoothly over his tautly muscled shoulders and the gold coin glittering against the bronzed column of his throat. Without looking, she could trace the deeply grooved lines of his face and know the way his eyes crinkled with silent laughter as he watched and listened to the children report on matters too important to wait even a moment longer.

Every word, every action was an assault on her senses that left her reeling in its wake. No, such foolishness was not even to be considered. That would be jumping out of the frying pan and into the fire, because Jason was not only a physically attractive man but one she could fall in love with all too easily.

Not necessarily true, her obstinate mind argued. She

wasn't some silly child, she was a grown woman and capable of ruling her emotions, and he didn't know that her prickly stand-offish charade wasn't genuine. What was more, he didn't care. She was his employee, nothing more. If he could have created a computer to do her job, he would have. Since he couldn't, he was stuck with her, as poorly equipped to do the job as he thought she was. In that fact lay the makings of an excellent contract.

Also, Miss Hawk had demanded more than just a husband. She had demanded a role pattern for the boys, and those four could be a hell-raising handful if they put their minds to it. Once, when Bobby Ray Spencer had thought to nominate himself for the role of husband and surrogate father, they had taken him swimming and accidentally tossed his clothes into a patch of poison ivy before remembering they had other important business elsewhere. But they respected and liked Jason, no contrived accidents would befall his person or possessions.

Furthermore, such a contract would involve no changes, no second man, no unknown risks, no possible mass murderers, and no one would be all that surprised. The village gossips would nod and wink and start counting months on their fingers. Then they would run out of fingers and toes to count on and still have nothing worth counting, she added with a certain malicious delight.

A new agreement with Jason would be the perfect answer to her problem, and his too. She could offer two for one—continued stability in his daughter's life and free use of the farm. More business was discussed in front of a roaring fire over a glass or two of smooth whisky, after a day of hunting or fishing than was ever successfully concluded in a stuffy boardroom. Tommie Staunton had known that, and so did Jason Reese. He had even suggested it, almost, when he had commented on what a perfect hideaway the farm was for a weary man.

Unaware of piercing blue eyes covertly scrutinising the play of emotions crossing her expressive face, Katie's tongue peeped out to moisten her soft lips. Tonight, when all the little ears were safely sleeping, she would propose a slight modification to their present arrangement. After something to soothe his weary mind, something warming and calming, something a hundred and twenty proof, she would skilfully nudge the conversation that way. Jason was a businessmen, he would quickly grasp the logic of her proposition, if it was presented properly. She had nothing to lose and a husband to gain. Miss Hawk wanted a bona fide man in her life; Katie would give her a knock-out, Jason Reese, six foot three inches of genuine man.

Katie glanced down at the ice-filled glasses and bottle of aged bourbon. What had seemed so simple a few hours earlier was becoming fraught with complications and questions. The idea was ludicrous. She was attempting a seduction. Proposing to Jason Reese was even more ridiculous than putting an ad in the paper.

Gnawing her underlip, she contemplated postponing the project for a day, to more carefully think out her strategy. She shook her head firmly. If she didn't do it now she never would. Taking a deep breath, she rapped on the closed study door.

One glance told her things were not going well. The desk was strewn with papers and schematic drawings, some had even spilled over on to the floor. His hair was rumpled and even now he was raking the rich walnut brown thickness with his fingers, something he did only when lost in troubled thought.

'I thought you might like a drop or two of something to settle your mind, Mr Reese.' The nearness of him struck her and she longed to smooth his ruffled hair and kiss his troubled mouth. She forced her lips into a firm line and riveted her eyes to the tray and silently ordered her mind to stick to business.

A glimmer of a smile lit Jason's face. He thought she had seemed somehow different tonight. This was the first time she had sought his company; perhaps patience was going to be rewarded.

Katie's heart skittered to a halt, then banged wildly against her ribs. Jason seemed genuinely surprised and pleased. She splashed lavish amounts of bourbon into the tumblers and reminded herself one more time that this was business and that the idea was to induce a relaxed and congenial atmosphere so Jason could appreciate the practicality of her proposition. She was not here to indulge in fantasies. There were times when a person simply enjoyed having someone near—nobody special, just somebody. If this was one of those times for Jason, so much the better. It would make him even more receptive to her proposal, if she could find the correct way to broach the subject.

She took the coward's way out and hid in the safety of the big chair, the width of the room acting as a buffer against his potent maleness. Rolling the glass nervously between her palms, she realised she didn't have the slightest idea of how to go about proposing a practical marriage. She started with a quick swallow of whisky and held her breath until it settled in a pool of warmth in the pit of her icy stomach. A second swallow helped even more. A third and the warmth spread to the tips of her trembling fingers.

She dared to peep at him through the fringe of her lowered lashes, then a tremor shook her body and senses as the implications of what she was proposing to do assailed her mind. Hastily, she stood and turned her back to him, concentrating on examining the spines of the books lining the wall.

'Mr Reese——' she looked over her shoulder at the man who filled the room with his presence, kindling her nerves and warming her blood, even as he leaned back in his chair, his dark head thrown back, his eyes half closed, savouring the taste of his drink, oblivious to her existence.

Katie swallowed her irritation with being so unimportant to him with a whisky chaser and plunged in. 'I would like to discuss a business proposition with you, sir. A purely business proposition.'

Jason nodded, his half-closed eyes lingering on the red bandana print butterfly appliquéd to her jeans, thinking, 'Lucky butterfly,' and of the many things he wanted to discuss with her, none of which pertained to business. A naughty couplet ran through his mind: 'Candy's dandy, but liquor's quicker.' Something to be kept in mind if all else failed.

'Our arrangement has worked well?' Katie stammered, mistaking his thoughtful silence for wary condescension.

'Yes,' Jason admitted. A smile softened the harsh contours of his face. It was working, if slowly. She was still determinedly formal and distant, but he was convinced that was more from habit and stubborn pride than anything else. And she was here. And there were times when she almost forgot to call him sir, almost looked at him, almost smiled at him. He was a patient man, and he wanted her in his life as well as his bed.

'Things are coming along,' he agreed.

Katie gulped the remnants of her drink and smiled at the floor. That was a good beginning.

A horrible thought flashed through her head. 'Mr Reese, is there a special lady in your life? You asked me the same thing once,' she hastened to remind him in defence of her unmannerly prying.

'Yes, I did, didn't I?' drawled Jason, wondering for the first time what kind of business they were discussing. 'The answer is no, no special lady.'

'Good,' Katie breathed without thinking. 'I mean, it

seems to me that what you need is a mother for Poppet, and since I find myself in need of a husband——' the words that had started out in such a rush to be said stuck in her throat and refused to budge.

An eternity of silence crawled by. She could not speak or force her eyes to meet his or command her feet to move. Mute and motionless, she waited for the world to end or the hills to swallow her.

Jason was on his feet, stalking her, anger hardening the firm line of his jaw and glittering in his eyes. 'Kathleen are you in trouble?'

'No, sir,' she insisted with a proud thrust of her chin, her own responding anger returning her power of speech. She knew exactly what kind of trouble he meant. 'I said business, Mr Reese, and that is exactly what I meant. A purely business proposition, a mutually beneficial arrangement, an open-ended, written contract which can be terminated by either party at any time. In exchange for the use of your last name I am offering you a lease on my property for entertaining and my services as a baby-sitter.'

The brittle fortress of her anger halted his relentless advance. Jason stared at her, unable to believe what he had heard. Clawing at his hair, he groaned and turned to the desk and poured a fresh drink.

'You are proposing to lease my services as a husband?' he asked, questioning his sanity as well as hers.

'No services, sir, in name only,' Katie insisted with a haughty edge to her voice equalling the angle of her chin. 'Temporarily.'

'Why?' he demanded.

'Ain't none of your-no-never-mind,' she retorted.

Gripping the edges of the desk, Jason took a deep breath. 'Kathleen, when a young woman proposes to me, even a temporary proposal, it most certainly is some of my'—he flung his hand in the air, searching for her pet phrase—'no-never-mind.'

'Yes, sir,' Katie admitted with a grudging shrug. Her lashes fluttered down, her mouth drooped in a pouting frown. She knew Jason well enough to know by the set of his jaw he was prepared to wait for the rest of eternity, if necessary, for an explanation. She did owe him one, and his brief flash of anger had been a warning, he wanted the truth.

'When Miss Hawk said to get reliable trasportation, I did. I sold the Tiffany lamp and bought the Bronco, it'll go through everything short of hell and high water. When she said to get visible means of support, I did. When she didn't like the first way, I found another. Now she says to get a husband.' She raised her eyes and faced him defiantly, her eyes darkening with a mixture of pain and pride and anger. 'I aim to. I figured to give you first chance, that's all.'

'First chance!' Jason roared.

'Yes, sir.' She refused to retreat in the face of his unexpected outrage and forced her trembling legs to stand their ground. 'I put an ad in the newspaper. I'm in a bit of a hurry.' Belatedly, she hid her left hand behind her back and crossed her fingers. The ad was as good as sent and she was in a hurry.

'Oh, my God!' Jason clawed at his hair and swore under his breath before abruptly turning his attention to the paper-strewn desk.

He had heard detailed accounts of Katie's brushes with Miss Hawk from the boys. As an interested listener he felt a measure of pity for the woman, who from his point of view was more often than not caught between a rock and a hard place, bureaucratic red tape and Katie's stiff-necked pride. If the woman had been hellbent on Katie's destruction, she could have done much more than strongly suggest a new line of work when she discovered Katie was working in a bar. Missouri had very clear-cut laws, the minimum drinking age was twenty-one, and court order or no court order, Katie had been eighteen at the time.

Jason glared at the papers he was stacking and shuffling. What had the woman said? Irrelevant, since Katie was convinced that she had said, 'Get a husband.' It was easier to re-programme an entire system than to get something out of Katie's head once it was in. His only hope was to reason with her.

'Kathleen, that's insane. You can't order a husband through the want ads like some kind of household gadget, any more than this Hawk woman can force you into a paper marriage. The court has already declared you a fit and able guardian. You receive no monies or other support from the state. She doesn't have a legal leg to stand on—they'd laugh her right out of a courtroom.'

Katie studied his clearly enunciated words and the unyielding set of his broad shoulders, and her nails bit into her palms. He had stated the simple, unvarnished truth as he saw it. She would spare him the further discomfort of making an outright refusal of her ridiculous offer and salvage the tag ends of her pride at the same time.

'No one is forcing anything, Mr Reese,' she said, her brows rising in a disdainful arch as she glided towards the door. 'I'm of an age to be thinking about such things, in case you hadn't noticed.' She smoothed her faded Levis over her thighs, intentionally outlining the feminine curves he remained blind to.

Her mouth curved in a bitter smile as she remembered the waitress and the way Jason's eyes had drifted over her body. He would never look at her that way. To him she was nothing more than a misshapen computer, programmed to kiss skinned knees and wash dirty faces. But she wasn't a computer, she was a flesh and blood woman. Why couldn't he see that?

'This house has been without a baby too long. A

newspaper ad is as logical a way as any to get what I want. Now, if you will excuse me, sir, morning does come early and I do have things to do.'

'Such as renting a husband?' Jason grated.

'Among other things,' she answered in a tone as frigid as his.

Their eyes met in a bitter clash of wills, one which Katie refused to lose. Her pride demanded a victory of some kind, no matter how minuscule. Head high, spine stiff, she swept from the room. She had won; he had looked away. Fleeing, she withheld the scalding tears burning in her throat and eyes until she had gained the safety of the upstairs hall. Her victory was ashes and the taste was bitter.

Katie completed the bedtime ritual by sealing Poppet's eyes before relinquishing the little one to her father, the normal ending to a normal Saturday. She had expected some repercussions in the wake of her temporary insanity and had spent much of the day calling herself six kinds of fool and seven kinds of idiot and trying to think of some excuse for her behaviour. Her nerves stretched near the breaking point waiting for Jason to announce his permanent departure. But he had carried on a perfectly normal day, dividing his time between work and play. He and the brood had fished and swum and played ball. He remained as oblivious to her as he ever had.

His actions confused her and made her wonder if she could have dreamed the whole thing. The awful sureness that she hadn't dreamed even one word clawed at her stomach and raked up fears of what must surely come. She had to escape the confines of the house and seek the solace of her hills. As quickly as possible, without appearing to do so, she fled to the moon-shadowed dancing floor.

Even the hills, brooding in the moonlight, seemed

disinclined to notice her. She closed her eyes to blot out their looming outline and her fear of losing the tiny corner of Jason's life she had held. She could not explain away last night by pretending that a tumbler of neat whisky had addled her senses. Neither would she risk another court battle with Miss Hawk. Her road was plainly marked, family first. Jason Reese was an outsider passing by on his way to somewhere else. The hills had warned her, but she'd been too much a fool to fool to listen.

'Kathleen!'

Her stomach knotted and twisted, sending out shock waves that shook her entire being. It was over.

'Yes, sir,' she whispered, keeping her back to him, her eyes to the hills.

'I've given our conversation of last night a great deal of thought, and I believe we can reach a mutually beneficial agreement.'

Her world flip-flopped crazily as the hills joined her heart in an exuberant clog dance. She threw her head back to see beyond the hills to the stars. Jason was saying yes. He was staying.

'There's no harm in discussing it.' Katie was stunned to realise that the calm, dispassionate voice was hers.

'You'll want a church wedding, of course.'

'No, sir. A stroll across the border will do just fine.' She shook her head jerkily. It hurt to so callously push aside the long-cherished dreams of a white gown and God's blessings and neighbour's good wishes. A real marriage, she reminded herself, demanded a real wedding. A business contract did not.

'If you're talking about a state border, that's a bit more than a stroll.'

A wry smile twisted her mouth. She had forgotten, he wouldn't know about border towns specialising in laundry-ticket marriages—in by ten, out by two— cleaned, pressed and married. Such towns were common knowledge among young people in a hurry.

She shrugged. 'An easy day trip.' It was more often a hasty night drive.

'I see.'

Her eyes misted with tears quickly blinked away. It was business and he was a businessman, how else should he sound?

'When?'

'At your convenience,' she matched his cool tone.

'Monday? The holiday Wednesday slows the entire week. Monday would be the best time for me.'

'Yes, of course.'

Katie wrapped her arms around her waist and closed her eyes to blot out the pain in her soul. They sounded like two strangers in a supermarket discussing cuts of meat: 'Would you like a chuck roast today? No, I think I'll have the chicken. There's nothing much happening, shall we get married and have pork chops instead?'

Buying a cut of meat or buying a husband, accounts had to be kept and payments made. The sooner done the less it hurt. She bit the tender inside of her lip, the pain and salty taste of blood keeping her firmly in touch with reality. 'Mr Fenton, my lawyer, can draw up the papers. Or your attorneys, if you prefer.'

'I prefer no attorneys. We're both adults, Kathleen. I foresee no complications.'

'No, sir. No complications.' Katie forced herself to turn and face the man who would be her husband in less than forty-eight hours. His face was as hard as his words, as unyielding as the hills he was studying.

'I don't want the little ones to know that this is business,' she whispered, her voice stumbling over the word her heart was growing to detest.

'The children least of all,' Jason agreed.

'We have a deal, then?' Chin high, Katie attempted a jaunty smile. When he nodded, she stuck out her hand. It was traditional to seal a business deal with a handshake.

His hand brushed over hers. The strong lean fingers leisurely traced a course along her arm to the hollow at the base of her throat to cup her chin. 'Proposals are usually sealed with a kiss.' Gently, he guided her mouth to his.

With skilled ease he parted her lips to taste the sweet moistness of her mouth as he drew her into the strength of his body. A searing fire swept through her veins, leaving an aching hunger she had never known before but which she knew instinctively only he could satisfy. Moaning softly, she offered her mouth for a deeper, more penetrating exploration.

Her arms twined around his neck, urging him to a more complete possession of her body trembling with a woman's primal need for completion. A shudder of ecstasy forced a muted cry from her lips as he cupped the swelling fullness of her breast in his hand. She cradled his head to her breasts. Swaying with the undulating rhythm of their pounding pulses, she surrendered to the timeless need of a woman for her man.

There was only Jason. The intoxicating male scent of him, the warm strength of him surrounding her, drugging her senses, pulling her even more deeply into the firm length of him. His mouth branded her as his, finding the thrusting swell of her breasts and laying claim to them and her.

They alone were the universe. Nothing else existed, only the two of them, freed of time and place, soaring to new and dizzying heights she had never imagined existed.

'Mr Reese, you all best get yourselves untangled real quick like, 'cause this gun is loaded and I'm a dead shot. Ain't no way I could miss at this range.'

Terror froze the scream in Katie's throat as she twisted to throw herself between Jason and the shadowed figure on the porch. There was a note of pleading in the low-pitched growl. Chance would regret shooting the man he had come to admire, but their father had put Katie in his care. He was the man of the house.

She struggled against Jason's superior strength pulling her aside. He had no way of knowing that the grim-faced boy with the levelled shotgun had been a man too long to be cajoled into submission. Any more than he would know that Chance never took more than two shells when he went squirrel hunting—two shots for two squirrels, enough for supper. Enough to kill a man.

Katie found herself trapped against Jason's side, his steel-hard fingers biting her waist, demanding her acquiescence. His eyes never left the deadly, blued steel aimed at his chest. Slowly he extended his arms, freeing her and moved directly into the path of fire.

'I've asked your sister to become my wife, and she has agreed.' His voice was as level and steady as the gun butted into Chance's shoulder.

The gun wavered, then righted itself. 'That right, Katie?'

'Yes,' she whispered, seeing only the cold steel glinting in the moonlight and the horror it could call into being.

His jaw clenching and unclenching, Chance studied Jason. He nodded once, then carefully eased the hammers down. 'I'll be pleased to call you brother, Mr Reese.' With no further explanation or any apology the boy slipped away as silently as he had come.

Katie held out her hand in a mute attempt to recall him. Chance, the one most like their father, was the gentle one, the peacemaker, slow to anger and quick to forgive. Her heart ached for the boy pushed to the brink of violence by what he saw as his duty.

'I'd forgotten how possessive the Staunton men are.'

Katie whirled to face the voice behind her. Moonlight threw his craggy face into sharp relief, making it look even more rough-hewn and stony. She moistened her lips still tingling with the imprint of his mouth, then retreated into the shadows of the porch to hide the pain reflected in her eyes.

'It's a family trait,' she answered, raising her chin to hide its trembling. The memory of their brief lovemaking exploded through her mind as she belatedly repaired her disarranged clothing. It could not have been as one-sided as Jason's cool, faintly mocking tone implied. She squeezed her eyes shut and gnawed the tender inside of her lip. She had to know.

'Was he here long?' she asked, allowing only a trace of curiosity to be heard.

'Not long,' Jason answered matter-of-factly. He had no idea of how long the boy had been there. He wanted to give her the answer she wanted to hear, his mountain wildcat, already in retreat and denying that she had responded with a hunger as deep and aching as his.

Katie's hope crumbled. Jason had seen Chance and set about convincing the boy that their marriage was the natural culmination of events in the surest, most logical way possible. It had been a most convincing performance. She had almost believed it herself.

Her chin angled. She was a fool, ten times a fool. If she had any sense she would order Jason Reese out of her house and life now, tonight, before he claimed what she had so willingly offered and would offer again when there was no boy with a gun to shock her back to reality.

There was her pride, however, and he had accepted her business proposition and reaffirmed that agreement. Honour demanded that she live up to her side of their bargain. The brood would never know her marriage was a business arrangement, and Jason Reese would never know it wasn't.

CHAPTER SIX

THE glitter of a playful sunbeam dancing across the heavy gold band holding her third finger captive drew Katie's attention from the roadside grasses rushing by. It was done. She was Mrs Jason Reese. A bored judge, between sentencing petty thieves, had ushered them into a dusty back room and, with his clerk as witness, pronounced them legally husband and wife. Not exactly a thing of beauty, but no force on earth could take the children from her now.

A heavy sigh forced its way past her lips.

'Tired?' Jason asked his silent bride. His eyes momentarily left the curving road ahead. He didn't know whether he wanted to take her in his arms and comfort her or shake her until her teeth rattled, so he did neither. Even though he had seen less doleful new widows.

'No, sir—no, Jay,' Katie amended hastily, shaking her head. The name Jay came hard to her tongue, it was a chopped-off sound that hung in the air waiting to be finished. She preferred Jason, which her soft drawl transformed into Jay-sin.

She bit her lip and commanded her face to smile at the man beside her. She knew she should be lighting candles and shouting thanksgivings to the high heavens, not moping with a long face. Jason Reese wasn't the villain in a potboiler melodrama. He hadn't threatened to foreclose the mortgage on the old plantation if she didn't give in to his dastardly will. Quite the contrary, she had propositioned him. It wasn't his fault that he'd struck a bargain and taken her at her word. The least she could do was be civil.

Her trembling underlip drooped in an uncivil pout. Her effort had gone unnoticed. His eyes had already returned to the road and his thoughts to elsewhere. Jason Reese! He wouldn't notice if she danced naked across the hood of his car, unless she had a computer glued to her navel, and then he'd only wonder if it was one of his or a competitor's product. Which was a good thing, she reminded herself, since she wasn't to be trusted.

Keeping her mind on business was going to be more difficult than she had imagined. Even the light kiss he had pressed on her lips when the magistrate had pronounced them man and wife had ignited her blood and left a craving for more. It had taken every ounce of will power and pride she possessed to remain unresponsive. What would it be like at home, where the presence of five other people, never far away, would demand more examples of marital bliss? She peeped out of the corner of her eye at his blatantly masculine profile, and a delicious shiver scampered down her spine. Perhaps, if he played the role long enough, pretense would become reality.

Not likely, she lectured silently, and she'd be well advised to get her head back to earth if she knew what was good for her. A kiss? What was a kiss? People were forever kissing everything from babies to old grannies. Unfortunately, Jason fitted neither category.

'I won't call you Jay,' she informed him, her underlip pushed out in a firm pout, her chin tilted up.

'Mr Reese would seem a bit formal now,' contended Jason, a glint of amusement twinkling in his eyes. Katie leading with her chin was Katie returning to normal.

'I mean to call you Jason,' she flared, glaring out of the window and knowing full well she was being argumentative for no good reason other than she felt like it.

The brood was waiting for them. Jeeter and Poppet,

stationed by the mail box, gave the hue and cry when the car was little more than a westerly-heading dust boll.

Katie stepped out of the rented car amid a virtual downpour of rice and good wishes, and found herself being swept off her feet and into Jason's arms, much to the delight of their audience. Her mind knew it was only business, but her arms didn't care. They encircled his neck and pulled her head to his shoulder. His breath teased her ear, followed by the lingering caress of his mouth brushing the sensitive nape of her neck, rekindling the flames of desire and sending them racing through her veins. She hid her face in his chest, surrounding herself completely with his maleness, hoping that their journey to the house would never end.

All too soon they were over the threshold and Jason was setting her free. She wanted to cry out: 'Look at me. Love me.' Pride won out, she stepped away from him smoothing her hair and dress and laughing a trifle shakily, as a new bride should.

'Come on, see what we did for you,' Poppet and Jeeter insisted, each tugging at a hand, leading Katie and Jason upstairs.

'See!' Beaming, Poppet swept the room that had been her bedroom with her hand. 'This is your room now, Daddy. Katie doesn't like having her things messed with, so all your clothes are in here,' she added knowledgeably as she opened a dresser drawer.

'But you sleep in here,' Jeeter bowed, and opened the connecting door and pointed towards Katie's bed.

'But—but—Poppet, you're afraid to sleep alone,' Katie babbled. She had not considered the possibility of the whispered planning that had gone on all day Sunday going in this disturbing direction, switching bedrooms.

'Katie's afraid to sleep alone,' Poppet corrected, repeating Katie's old lie with a grave nod. 'And she cuddles.' She shrieked the last word and succumbed to a fit of giggles.

'Wonderful,' Jason murmured, surrounding Katie's waist with his hands as he nibbled her ear. 'I like to cuddle too, especially with soft, warm, sweet-tasting wives.'

Poppet giggled behind her hands while Katie waged war with herself. She forced her mind to repeat the words that had become a charm, it was only business. The little ones had to be convinced. Jason was playing a role for the children. She was not a child; it was only business. She repeated the spell to ward off the effects of the man bedevilling her senses. The lingering caress of his hands was only business. The way he held her sheltered in the strength of his hard, masculine body was only business. It was only business, nothing more.

'Wait till you all see what else we done,' Jeeter crowed. 'Wait till you all see what Chance did!'

'That'll be enough, boy,' Emma Parks, the house-keeper of Katie's childhood recalled to duty for the day, warned from the hallway, as she aimed a loving swat at Jeeter bouncing past. 'Chance'll do his own telling and showing. But it truly is something worth crowing about, I'll tell you all that much.'

Her wide smile lit on Jason and screwed itself into a righteous scowl. 'Congratulations, Mr Reese, you got yourself a real lady there—but then I reckon you know that.' She drew her short, thick body into a grim exclamation point of disapproval for such goings-on. A warning that this outlander had better know that her Baby Girl, as she had always called Katie, was a lady if he valued life and limb.

'My sweet lady,' murmured Jason, his voice a husky whisper in Katie's ear that soothed the old woman's doubts about their instant marriage and did everything but soothe Katie.

Emma Parks sounded a deep, 'Harrumph!' in her

throat and wiped her hands on her apron, appeased for the moment by the words and the man.

'And where might it be, Miss Katie Claire, that folks eat their dessert before their proper supper? I been hearing about that one all day,' she accused with a sharp thrust of her chins.

'The Fugimingo Islands, isn't it, Kathleen?' asked Jason, burying the last of Emma's doubts with a crooked grin so full of playful mischief even his eyes were dancing with impish delight.

'I believe so,' Katie murmured, allowing herself to be drawn into the circle of his arms, wondering if she could escape unscathed, from the web of deception she had begun and he was so skillfully weaving around them.

'Ah, get on with you, the pair of you! Lucky for me, my brain ain't so ossified as you'd like to think. And you, girl,' the old woman snapped the skirt of her apron at Katie, 'you ain't even got the good grace to cross your fingers any more before telling an old lady a whopper like that. And you, Mr Jay, you're just as bad, egging her on that way.'

Katie stared at the broad back leading their way downstairs to the rest of the secret plans the brood had made and carried out. Jason's fatal charm had already worked its magic. In a matter of minutes he had changed a snarling tigress intent on protecting her cub into a purring pussycat. He was Mr Jay and she was 'girl'. He was protective while she was spinning tales. It wasn't fair.

She transferred her frustration to its rightful owner, Jason Reese, and found him gazing down at her, a hint of amusement tugging at his firm mouth and lurking in his eyes. He was very pleased with his performance. Katie accepted his mocking challenge with a haughty tilt of her chin. Matching his public performances would be no problem, she had only to do what came naturally. It was their private moments with only her crumbling will power and pride for defences that she feared.

The brood's carefully planned surprise was modelled after the marriage dances captured in the sepia-toned photographs of an earlier era. The stereo and speakers, brought outside for the occasion, replaced the bearded fiddlers and banjo pickers on the back porch. A very respectable wedding feast complete with tiered cake was spread over linen-covered planks and saw-horses. Festive crêpe paper streamers wound their way down porch posts and around railings. Five cautiously proud children silently waited for their verdict.

'It's beautiful. Lovely,' Katie complimented the line-up of children and Mrs Parks hovering in the background. A surge of emotion prevented her saying more. Wordlessly, she hugged and kissed first Poppet, then each of the boys in turn, ending with Mrs Parks, who returned her to Jason.

'Here now,' Emma Parks coached, shoving Chance forward as she dabbed at her eyes with a handy apron corner.

'I—we did something for you,' Chance muttered. Shoving his hands in his pockets, he managed to look equally embarrassed and proud as he swaggered a few feet and jerked his head towards the dancing floor. 'Seemed fitting. Congratulations.'

Tears blurred Katie's vision. Chance, the artisan, hadn't stinted his labour or talent for whittling. Cut into the paving stone were her and Jason's intertwined initials and the date surrounded by the beginnings of a border of grape clusters and leaves. It was a gift that would outlast the occasion it marked by a century.

'I figured I had all summer to cut them deeper. Rock's harder than wood,' Chance shrugged, dismissing his work and the care that had gone into it.

His hands edged out of his pockets as his eyes crept

up to Jason's, hesitantly asking him to accept his gift as
it was intended, a peace-offering. Jason did, with a
broad smile and a firm handshake, both eagerly
returned.

'Musicians, if you please,' Jason called to Bo and
Rocky stationed on either side of the stereo turntable.

'Yes, sir!' Both boys jumped to obey, bowing to each
other and flooding the air with the melody of a
romantic ballad which Emma Parks quickly lowered to
a less ear-splitting level.

'Mrs Reese, may I have this dance?' Smiling, Jason
gathered Katie in his arms, the gentle but firm pressure
of his hand on the small of her back leading her into the
music.

For a moment Katie's pride resisted, reminding her
that this too was only business and would last no longer
than the music. But the sweet-sad melody was
whispering what her heart felt and ached to hear and
Jason was holding her.

The hand she had put out to hold him away slipped
from his shoulder to caress the back of his neck while
the slow, sensual pulse of the music drew her head to
his shoulder. The sweet ache of touching him and being
in his arms filled her. Jason was her mountain, he was
the storm that could make her desert bloom. She clung
to him, lost in the pleasure of the perfect way their
swaying bodies fitted together. The rounded thrust of
her breasts brushing the hard wall of his broad chest
responded, the nipples hardening, becoming even more
achingly sensitive. The pressure of his hard, masculine
length, the feel of his firm male thighs, so close she
could feel the warmth of him, enveloped her in a
tingling glow. She wanted to stay in his arms for ever,
surrounded by him, her senses filled with him.

The music ended, drawing from her a soft moan that
left her lips parted and trembling, inviting Jason's
possession. Catching her face in the frame of his hands,

he lowered his mouth to cover hers in a firm yet tender promise that this was only the beginning. A promise delayed by a whispered chorus of drawn-out, 'Wow!' that reminded them they were far from being alone.

They changed partners for the next dance, Jason claiming first Poppet and then Emma Parks while Katie was handed from boy to boy. The boys, realising possibly for the first time that Katie was one of those most mystifying of creatures, a woman, were overcome with the galloping bashfuls. They were no longer sure of where they should or safely could touch her or that she might not break. She knew they would recover rapidly, possibly by morning when she would once again be just Katie. Poppet too was seeing Katie in a new way, and the fear mirrored in those blue eyes was in no way humorous.

During a break in the music, Katie claimed Poppet's hand.

'Will you share my flowers? Will you be my bridesmaid?' Katie asked.

Staring at her shoes, Poppet nodded an uncertain little yes, far different from her usual exuberant acceptance of anything that was Katie's.

'We'll have to find a pin.' Katie coaxed the little one to the kitchen and set her up on the table. She plucked one of the pale yellow roses from her corsage, disturbing its carefully balanced arrangement. A child was more important than a pretty posy.

'What's wrong, little one?' Katie asked softly. Poppet's chin had drooped so far into her chest she didn't see the offered rose.

'Do I have to call you Mama now?' The words were barely audible and shaky.

'Oh no. No,' Katie whispered, stroking the child's cheek. Nasty witches and evil stepmothers had suddenly left their fairy tales and come too close to possible reality for the little one's comfort. 'I'm just Katie. I'm still just Katie. And I hope you still want me to be your Katie, because I oh, so very much want you to keep on being my Poppet.'

Hunching her shoulders, Poppet guarded her misery, which was real and not easily shared. 'Even if you have your own baby Poppet to love?'

'Yes.' Katie gathered the child in her arms. 'You're Poppet. There'll never be another Poppet for me. You're special. No one could ever take your place in my heart, because I love you, and that's an always and forever kind of loving.'

'Even if I still miss my real mommy just a little bit?' Poppet asked, her fear that Katie might say no keeping her stiff and resistant to Katie's arms.

'Oh, Poppet, mommies are very special. They're a great big always and forever love. You just keep on loving her a whole lot. And she won't mind if you love me too, because mommies know little girls have room in their hearts for lots of people, just like lots of people have room for them.'

'I love you, Katie,' Poppet whispered, wrapping her arms around Katie's neck.

'And I love you,' Katie whispered back, returning the tightening hug.

'Can I still be your bridesmaid?' asked Poppet, her world righting itself and her enthusiasm creeping back.

'I'd like that,' Katie assured her.

'Can the father of the bridesmaid pin on her corsage?' Jason, who had watched and heard, asked huskily.

'I think he should,' Katie volunteered, moving away from Poppet and offering him the rose.

Taking the flower and her hand, Jason brought Katie back to be with them. 'Now, where does this go?' he asked, testing positions on Poppet's bodice.

'Over my heart, Daddy,' Poppet informed him.

The rose attached, Jason scooped the little girl up in his arms and balanced her on one hip. His free arm circled Katie's waist and drew her to his side. 'I have two beautiful women,' he told Poppet, and kissed her cheek. 'Beautiful,' he repeated to Katie, his mouth brushing hers, then returning to claim it more thoroughly.

'Ah, jeez!' an adolescent male voice groaned. 'We're out here starving and they're in there necking again!'

Katie rested her forehead on Jason's shoulder, savouring the lingering warmth of his kiss. There was no way, not a chance in a million, she could confuse fantasy and reality, not with the quantity and quality of chaperons they had.

The celebration was over and the little ones safely abed. Katie shivered in the night air, still and heavy with July heat. Rocking back and forth, cradled in her own arms, she raised a mute cry as ancient as the watching hills. What had she done?

'There you are.' Jason slipped strong arms around her waist and nibbled on the nape of her neck. 'I told Emma you'd be out here, counting your hills, making sure they'd all still be standing.'

Katie stiffened in his arms, her injured pride screeching its condemnation of her foolish heart for its moment of hope, for forgetting it was only business. They still had an audience, the play must go on for a while longer.

'Never doubted it for a minute, Mr Jay,' Emma Parks chortled. 'We both know this child, and those ol' hills have put their mark on her. Why, when she was no bigger than a tadpole she'd go off for hours on end just walking and talking and listening to those hills.'

'What do they say tonight?' Jason crooned, the intoxicating warmth of his breath brushing her ear.

'Beware of tall, dark strangers,' Katie parried, twisting free of his bemusing embrace, adding a sliver of laughter to assure their audience of one that it was a small joke, a private password between husband and wife.

'Tall and handsome, but no stranger, praise the Lord,' the old woman exulted. 'My Baby Girl went off and got herself married—I can't hardly believe it! Why, it seems like only the other day you was swiping cookies and getting your bottom blistered for your troubles, and now you're a married woman.' She sighed and shook her head at the spinning whirligig time had become. 'Still say it ain't right, you not getting away for a bit. Nothing would please me more than looking after those babies for a week or two. Got nothing better to do.'

'Thank you, Mrs Parks, but I don't want any of the little ones to feel left out.' With a smile Katie repeated her hastily contrived excuse for not taking a honeymoon.

Emma Parks sounded her bullfrog snort. 'They ain't worried about being pushed out—they're too happy about being put together. Why, if those boys could choose a man for you it would be Mr Jay. And that Poppet—why, the only reason the sun gets up of a morning is 'cause you tell it to. You got no worries there, girl.'

'Oh, rattle, rattle, Emma,' she chided herself suddenly. 'Get yourself to bed, give these young folks some privacy. I made you some coffee, honey, just the way you like it.'

'Thank you, again, Mrs Parks,' whispered Katie, wrapping the woman in a hug and kissing her time worn cheek. 'For everything.'

'Why, child,' Emma protested, catching Katie's face in her hands, 'I'd have been put off to no end if you hadn't asked. I only got one regret, that your sweet mama ain't here to see our Baby Girl and what a fine lady she turned out to be. And what a good man she got. A good man.' Raising the hem of her apron, she dabbed at Katie's moist eyes. 'Now, you get to hugging and kissing on the one you should be carrying on with. Mr Jay, you get on over here and take your wife to home, in your arms, where she belongs.'

She heaved a tremendous sigh of contentment and beamed her approval when Jason came as bid and stood behind his bride.

His hands spreading possessively over her abdomen turned Katie's stomach to butterflies and her bones to quivering jelly. The charm of reciting in her mind that this was only business lost its power. Her mind was much too busy being aware of Jason's closeness, so close she could feel the warmth of his breath on her ear right down to her toes, to be bothered with any recitation.

'There is one other thing, Mr Jay,' Emma Parks warned, 'this here girl is pure Staunton, through and through—hard-headed. You'd best take a firm hand right now or she'll be thinking on putting that wedding ring through your nose!'

Jason's answer was a throaty chuckle barely begun when Katie found herself being turned and pulled into the hard length of his body.

Her hands came up instinctively to spread against the unyielding wall of his chest. Her feeble protest served only to arch her shoulders and make her lips more readily accessible to the bruising demand of his mouth. Her murmur of denial melted into an engulfing tidal wave that swept her arms up to curl around his neck and mould her trembling body to his. His hands moved from her shoulders to make a leisurely journey to the curve of her hips.

Assured of her response, his mouth wandered to taste the curve of her face, the line of her jaw and the sensitive hollow behind her ear, turning her blood to liquid fire. Caught up in the sensual flood he had unleashed, Katie guided his head to the swell of her breasts, the nipples tautly erect and thrusting forward in welcome.

From a distance came a smothered cackle of laughter and the whispering swish of a screen door opening and closing. In an instant Katie tore free, a new flood of emotion battering her senses. Backing away, she scrubbed her mouth with the back of her hand in a futile attempt to erase the still tingling memory of Jason's mouth crushing hers. Through a haze of tears she watched him warily, her breath coming in short, panting gasps. To her shame she had forgotten it was only business.

'Your coffee, Mrs Reese,' growled Jason, frustrated by this game of hot and cold she played so well. Catching her wrists in an iron grip, he unceremoniously jerked her back to him. 'We mustn't disappoint Mrs Parks,' he grated in her ear.

Not trusting her voice, Katie allowed her lips to curve in a bitter smile. How easily, how completely he aroused her, all the while listening and waiting for Mrs Parks to leave, but who might still pop back out necessitating an encore performance.

She would not be allowed to damage his carefully planned production at this stage. For it had become his creation. She had proposed a half-baked scheme and he, with his logical computer mind, had calculated the problems and solutions and produced an outstanding plan. He had located the town, the lab for the required blood tests, the willing magistrate. He had rented the car, bought the ring and even remembered flowers, the corsage of creamy roses and gypsophila she had shared with Poppet and Mrs Parks had lovingly wrapped in tissue and refrigerated to keep. He had planned and carried out their charade of a wedding with the same cold logic he used to solve all problems.

Her lashes sank to brush her cheeks and protect her from his chilled gaze. She was a new acquisition and must perform acceptably or be discarded as ruthlessly as any unprofitable business venture. Nodding her understanding of this bitter knowledge, she allowed him to lead her to the wicker settee.

She huddled in a corner, as far from Jason as possible. A single tear quivered on the tip of her lowered lashes. She would learn, she vowed, to play at love as effortlessly as he did, or at least make him think she had.

When his hand brushed her lowered chin she flinched and crowded even further into the corner. One word, one touch and she would beg him to make love to her, no matter what his motive.

'Kathleen.'

'Yes, sir—yes, Jason,' she hastily amended her slip of the tongue.

Anger darkened his face already shadowed by the elusive moon. 'You'd do anything, wouldn't you?' he rasped, his steel hard fingers biting her shoulders. 'Anything to keep those boys. You'd even sell yourself to a man you despise?'

'Yes,' she hissed, pouncing on the chance to inflict wounds as bitter as those she bore. 'I'll do anything to keep what's mine!'

'And if I decide to exercise my connubial rights, Mrs Reese, what then?' he taunted.

Her sharp intake of breath tore the still air. He laughed, a hollow, mirthless sound and pushed her away. 'Go to bed,' he growled, 'before I do something we'll both regret.'

Thoroughly miserable, Katie stared up at the ceiling. Tired, she could not will sleep to come. Exhausted, she could not force her mind to rest. She turned on her side, brushing her arm against her breast, aching and feverish with want. A sob caught in her throat for the Louisiana Bride's marriage bed, Katie Staunton's marriage bed, a bed so wide and soft and lonely.

She heard a creak, the loose board at the top of the backstairs, then another, closer. Jason was coming to bed. Her heart pounded wildly, its beat filling her head with frenzied thoughts. What if he made good his threat to claim his legal rights as her husband?

She jerked the sheet up to her chin. The only key that fitted both doors to her bedroom was in the left-hand handkerchief drawer of the dresser. She still had time. Carefully she eased one foot out of bed, then snatched it back. There was no way she could get to the dresser and both doors without him hearing. She would be safer if she pretended to be asleep.

She closed her eyes and held her breath, hoping to simulate the shallow breathing of a sleeper. If he tried getting into her bed she'd try reason first. If reason failed she would fight, kick, bite, hit, put a knee right where her mama had always told her to if the need arose. She'd leave no doubt in Jason Reese's mind as to the limits of their arrangement.

Her breath caught in her throat. He was at Poppet's door. She heard the door open, then close, and his footsteps continue. Her heart joined her suspended respiration. He was at her door. She raised the sheet to the level of her ears, only her eyes remained uncovered. If he tried moving that sheet she'd bite him! Human bites were dangerous. She'd chomp him up so hard it would take a whole team of doctors just to sew him back together and it would take him a year to recover from the tetanus shots.

Her chin sagged to rest on her clenched hands. She recognised the metallic click of the latch to the door of what was now his bedroom. She was safe, safe and vaguely disappointed.

She listened to the sounds of Jason undressing and the brass bed creak its protest to his weight. Her heart thudded in the silence and then lurched as the bedsprings squeaked and his bare feet padded across the room.

Moving only her eyes, she watched the connecting door. Cautiously, she inched her hand out until it touched the cool, solid form of her alarm clock. If he came that way she would bash him over the head before he knew what was happening.

The sliver of light visible under the door was snuffed out and the muffled footsteps retreated. Jason had turned out the lights and had gone to bed.

Katie buried her face in her pillow and quietly cried herself to sleep.

Groggy, Katie pushed her way to consciousness. Sleep, when it had come, had been heavy and still resisted her efforts to shake loose its embrace. Pushing up on her elbows, she cupped her chin in her hands and sleepily surveyed the familiar room.

She swore, a single explosive syllable that propelled her from the bed. Skinning out of her nightgown, she grabbed cut-offs and tee-shirt. Pausing only to fish her shoes out from under the bed, splash cold water on her face and run a brush through her sleep tangled hair, she sprinted for the steps and the kitchen below. She didn't need an alarm clock to tell her she'd overslept; the sun was too high and the house too quiet.

'Good morning, sleepyhead. Coffee's over there.' Jason, his long frame draped over a chair tilted back from the table, greeted her sudden, dishevelled appearance with an indulgent smile and a directing hand.

'I sent Emma with them,' he answered before she could ask. 'I turned off your alarm. You needed the sleep and we needed to talk, privately.'

'I'll thank you to not do that again,' Katie told him, her voice foggy with sleep, her stiffened spine showing her disapproval. 'We show up every morning, rain or shine, sick or healthy.'

'They did, and they will. You did not. You will not.'

'I'll do as I damn well please!' Katie flared, whirling to face the man who thought to dominate her as easily as he dominated all else.

'Sit down, Kathleen,' Jason ordered, his voice a low growl allowing no argument.

'I'm fine right here,' she parried, wedging herself more firmly into the L of the kitchen counter. Yesterday had taught her one thing, distance was a necessity.

She shrugged. Keeping her eyes resolutely focused on anything that wasn't Jason, she strolled around the room, stopping to test the taps—little drips all added up; to make sure the screen door was tightly closed, flies needed no more than a crack to invite themselves inside; to poke her head in the refrigerator—the little ones inhaled milk at an astounding rate. She ripped off the June leaf of the calendar and dropped it in the waste basket before slipping into the chair opposite the one he had indicated.

She was sitting. Not because he had ordered it or because his anger-tempered eyes warned that he was capable of enforcing that order, but because she wanted to sit.

'Continue to act like a child and I'll be forced to treat you like one,' Jason warned. 'Defy me again and I'll turn that shapely bottom of yours over my knee and spank it!' He had never raised a hand to a woman, felt only contempt for men who did, but even a patient man had limits.

'You wouldn't dare,' Katie huffed.

'Wouldn't I?' Jason challenged.

'You try beating on me, Mr Jason Reese, and I'll give you what for!' Katie promised with a flash of mountain temper.

She shook her head warily, denying what she read in the harsh lines of his face and saw glittering dangerously in his eyes. She gripped the edge of the round oak table, preparing for instant flight. Not only would he turn her bottom side up and paddle her behind, he would do so joyfully and thoroughly.

'No one has put a hand to me since I was ten years old,' she hissed, edging out of the chair while calculating the distance to the back door.

'A grievous tactical error,' grated Jason, unwinding his length from the chair with sensual male grace. This might not only be gratifying but enjoyable as well.

Flinging away from the table, Katie scrambled for the door, narrowly evading his arms. She vaulted the porch rail and landed running for the safety of the overgrown orchard, a well-remembered childhood escape route. She had only to reach the north-east corner where the woven wire fence was down to quickly lose herself in the encroaching brush. Emma Parks had never been able to find her when she hid, neither would Jason. In an hour or so Mrs Parks would return with the children and she would be free to go home. No one would wonder, for as Emma had said, Katie was given to solitary wandering. Nothing would be more natural than Katie Staunton sharing the joy of her wedding with her hills. And not even Jason Reese would dare make good his threat with six witnesses present.

She ventured a backward glance and to her horror saw that not only was he pursuing her but closing the distance between them and angling east, anticipating her route. She veered west and hoped she could reach and scramble over the wire before he could reach her.

In the split second allowed her between feeling her foot slip into the grass-hidden hole and sprawling earthward, Katie lamented the stupidity of a certain ignorant hillbilly too dumb to remember where the stump of a dead apple tree had been chopped and burnt out.

She scrambled up the slight incline on all fours, oblivious to everything except the adrenalin-induced obsession to escape. An iron-hard band encircled her waist and hauled her to her feet—Jason's arm. Twisting, an animal growl welling in her throat, she lashed out blindly, her arms and legs flailing in an attempt to strike any part of him.

Her uninjured foot connected solidly with his shin and brought forth a yelp of agony. Exulted, her roused blood singing, Katie threw herself at him, knocking him off balance, sending them both tumbling through the thick unkempt grass, her legs wrapped around his, her fists never ceasing the rain of blows aimed at his head and shoulders.

Each blow was vengeance extracted: For calling her a child. For charming the boys. For charming Emma Parks so effortlessly. For walking into her life. For turning her life upside down. For remaining so blind to her. For not loving her as she loved him.

Each blow was accompanied by a sob of frustration, for the battle she could not win, did not want to win, had to win. They stopped rolling. Crushed beneath the weight of his body, Katie continued her futile war until first her legs were taken captive and then her hands pulled away until they too were helpless. Panting, mutely shaking her head, she continued to deny—she no longer knew what.

'Katie. Katie,' he whispered. Pulling her hands together over her head, he locked them under the restraint of a single hand. Tenderly, he brushed the tangled curtain of hair from her face. 'I'm not the whole world, Katie, you don't have to fight me too. Don't you know that?'

Her eyes filled with tears. She did have to fight. If she didn't she would be lost in a whirlwind she could not control. She closed her eyes, squeezing them tight, and bit him, her teeth sinking deep into the fleshy part of his hand.

Multi-coloured fireworks exploded in her head as it

was snapped to one side by the stinging bite of his open-handed slap.

Suddenly she was free and scuttling for the protection of a nearby apple tree as they both retreated from the violence they had wrought.

'I'm going to have a swollen lip,' Katie complained as she gingerly explored the minimal damage to the side of her face with the tips of her fingers and tongue.

'To match my swollen hand.' Jason offered the bloodied evidence, a swelling curve of toothmarks extending from the base of his forefinger to the root of his thumb.

'I'm sorry,' Katie whispered, her eyes filling with contrite tears.

'You can't cage a wild thing,' murmured Jason, more to himself than to her, turning back to the house.

'Jason—Jason!' Katie scrambled to her feet and trotted after him. 'I'm hard-headed,' she told his back. 'Too independent for my own good. My daddy was forever telling me I'd best stuff my temper in my back pocket and keep it there.'

He turned to face her, the wry smile tugging at the corner of his mouth unable to reach the clouded depths of his eyes. Katie lowered her gaze, hunching her shoulders to protect against what she saw.

'No man in his right mind would saddle himself with a woman who does nothing but argue and beat him.' She spared him the cost of saying what she knew. 'Especially one he doesn't much care for and who keeps forgetting she did the asking.'

He smoothed the hair away from her face and tucked it behind her ears before cupping her chin in the strength of his hands and raising her face to meet his.

'I'll make your prison as pleasant as possible,' he promised. That was what he intended to do, cage her and hope she would become so accustomed to the comforts of her cage she would learn to love captivity and her captor.

CHAPTER SEVEN

KATIE hid in the shadow of an ancient oak, hugging her bare legs, her chin morosely resting on her knees. She tore a handful of grass from the soil and studied the mass of tangled roots. Poor pale things, dying but still stubbornly clutching the dirt caught in their matted web. She hurled the clod and watched in fall and bounce to a standstill, its stubborn roots still clinging to their illusion of life, too ignorant to know grass couldn't live when it had been torn up and thrown away. As ignorant as she was, still clinging to the hope that Jason would change illusion to reality.

Ignorant, because he had left no doubt as to which was which. His words had been clearly spoken and easily understood, even by a hard-headed hillbilly girl. They had made a bargain, a bad bargain, but a bargain none the less and one which would remain in effect until he dictated otherwise.

As agreed, he had given her the protection of his name; now she would live up to her side of their bargain. She was to be mother to his child and charming hostess to his guests. He wanted nothing more and would accept nothing less.

The day after the Fourth of July had seen an invasion that set the county agog. An army of workmen swarmed over the house, outbuildings and grounds, digging, cutting, tearing, hacking, scraping, pounding, banging until the old house was a showcase worthy of displaying the wife of Jason Reese.

The county's eyes saw what they were intended to see, that Katie Claire Staunton hadn't only hooked herself a rich man but one so crazy in love that nothing was too good for the new Mrs Reese. The county saw the illusion, Katie knew the reality. The renovated house, the bottomless checking account, even Emma Parks coaxed out of retirement; the highly visible and costly proofs of a man enamoured was a carefully calculated business ploy. She was an investment, his new hospitality centre, a comfortable place to wine and dine business associates and customers, nothing more.

Not that she hadn't benefited from their bargain. Miss Hawk, hearing the gossip, had come for a surprise snoop and left simpering congratulations. She no longer had to appliqué hearts or flowers or butterflies on blue jeans to conceal holes. She no longer had to worry about temperamental plumbing or running out of money for fuel before she ran out of winter. Their business arrangement had given her everything she could possibly want except one thing, the thing she craved most—Jason Reese. He had not been a part of their bargain.

Katie stood, brushing away the solitude of the hills. It was time to go back to the house and smile and make appropriate noises. It was time to listen to Jake Selby explaining what repairs had been done and what remained to be done. It was time to face Emma Parks, that sharp-eyed, sharp-eared, old student of human folly, who was already aware that not all was as it appeared on the surface. It was Friday evening, time for Jason to come home. Time to face the torment of seeing and hearing and being touched by Jason and know it was only business and the illusion would never become reality.

There was something brewing, nothing Katie could quite put her finger on, just something. The little ones were up to something and very pleased with themselves. It was evident in the surreptitious glances, the smothered giggles, the joggling elbows, the conscious effort of all five children to be completely natural and walk, not run out of Tara's main lodge.

Jason sensed it too. He reflected their contagious anticipation when he scooped Poppet up and tossed her in the air. 'What filled your giggle box so full?'

'Nothing,' giggled Poppet, squirming free of his embrace to grab Jeeter's hand and race across the parking lot to the truck.

The older three jammed their hands into their pockets and discreetly lengthened their stride, leaving Jason and Katie to follow at their leisure.

'Secrets?' Jason's hand captured Katie's neck, his fingers lightly caressing the tensed muscles of her neck.

Katie shrugged and turned down the corners of her mouth, commanding her head to ignore the tingling signals of pleasure his hand on her neck was creating and telegraphing to all her body. There was nothing personal in his touch. It was a necessary part of the game they were playing, and the sooner her hard head understood that the better.

She ducked away, pretending to search her bag for the truck keys. 'Got 'em! Sneaky little critters keep trying to hide,' she babbled, jingling the keys on their chain.

Jason's gaze travelled from the keys Katie was rattling to Chance. 'You got it.' He grinned at the boy, satisfied he'd discovered their secret.

'Yup!' Sixteen years and four days old, Chance ducked his head and selfconsciously dug his passport to wheeled adulthood, his newly won driver's licence, from his back pocket.

'In that case, home, Charles.' Reclaiming Katie's neck, Jason tossed the keys to Chance and guided Katie to the passenger side. His motioning thumb ordered the younger four to the back seat. Tonight he was sitting by Katie, a Katie not distracted with driving.

Trapped, Chance on her left and Jason on her right,

Katie couldn't call on her first line of defence, distance. They were jammed together with Jason's left arm absentmindedly draped over her shoulder. His fingers, tracing lazy circles on her skin, toying with the pencil-slim strap of her mint green sun-dress, did crazy things to her pulse and breathing. She was acutely aware of the firm masculine length of his body pressed against her, the warmth of him igniting every nerve ending, even those not in close contact. The musky scent of his cologne mingling with his own male scent filled her nostrils and bemused her mind.

She moistened her dry lips with the tip of her tongue and peeped up at him through the thick fringe of her lashes. His rough-hewn face was impassive and remote, his eyes half-closed with thought. He didn't know what he was doing to her. He didn't know, but she did, and she had to do something fast.

'Chance!' Katie lurched forward and stuffed her handbag into the narrow space opened between her and Jason, alleviating one distraction. 'You did everything but take that corner on two wheels. Slow down!' She pried Jason's fingers from her shoulder and twining hers through his raised his arm to the back of the seat and kept it there. Not a total victory over his disturbing influence but at least an armed truce.

Chance, who had actually turned the corner with exemplary caution, scowled at Katie, ready to defend his driving skill. The sight of his normally unflappable sister seemingly ready to burst into tears at any moment, her hand gripping Jason's so tightly her knuckles were white, cooled his heated pride. He growled something sounding suspiciously like, 'Women!' deep in his throat and slowed to ten miles under the speed limit.

'Do we have time to look things over before supper?' Jason asked Emma Parks, who had rushed out flapping her apron in welcome at the first sight of them.

'Well now, ain't that something?' drawled Emma, wrapping her hands in her apron as she conducted them to the kitchen. 'And me wanting a word with you on the very subject, Mr Jay. About supper. It's carload night at the drive-in tonight and a triple creature feature at that, so I've got tacos ready for the children's supper. We've got to get over there early—that movie lot fills up quick on a bargain night. But I've got steaks laid out for you two and potatoes baking in the oven. I figured to give the youngsters a night out and you all a nice romantic evening at home, alone.'

Katie gaped at the old woman beaming her smirking, self-satisfied leer at Jason. The brood's secret was the removal of her second major defence, then, carried out under the guidance and connivance of Emma Parks.

'I can't think of anything more enjoyable,' Jason agreed, a slow smile spreading to crinkle the corners of his eyes. 'Except, perhaps, a bottle of wine to add a glow to the candlelight.'

'No sooner said than done.' Emma threw open the refrigerator door and produced a bottle of wine. 'Chilled and waiting.'

Jason nodded appreciatively. 'From now on, Emma, you may plan all my seductions.'

'Mr Jay, ain't you something, though!' cackled Emma as she patted Katie's shoulder. 'Help me set the table, honey. It'll get us out of your way that much sooner.'

'Mrs Parks,' Katie warned, dumping an armload of plates on the dining-room table. 'You know how I feel about horror movies. They're not fit for children to see.'

Emma Parks sounded her bullfrog snort. 'They ain't horror pictures, they ain't nothing 'cept old monster movies. The only tears they're going to bring on is when the kids get to laughing too hard. They're so phoney the critters' strings show.'

'Still, you should have asked me.'

Emma turned, her eyes snapping her indignation, her fists dug into her ample hips. 'So you could think up half a dozen reasons why they couldn't go or you had to go with them. Girl, you ain't got enough sense to pound sand down a rat hole!'

'I for one have never understood the logic of wanting to pound sand down a rat hole,' blustered Katie.

'To keep the rat to home, Mrs Reese.' Emma bobbed her head and glared back at Katie.

'Well,' Katie sniffed, 'if I ever find a rat I want to keep at home, I shall certainly pound sand down his rat hole.'

'You just do that, honey. Quick-like!' Emma began dropping plates on the table. 'Separate bedrooms! I never heard of such goings-on in all my born days. If a man can't find something warm and soft and loving curled up in his own bed, he'll go looking—looking and finding, and you won't have nobody to blame 'cept you.'

Emma's sharp dart struck its target and twisted painfully. The image of Jason making love to another woman haunted Katie. She told herself that what he did the five nights a week he wasn't with her was none of her concern and that his complete indifference to her as a woman simplified matters.

She comforted herself with the knowledge that the investment Jason had in his hospitality centre was large and would necessitate a long term of amortisation. She raged at herself for being unable to kill the bud of hope that given enough time Jason would learn to love her. She was thoroughly miserable and knew the only torture worse than the one she was experiencing would be when he ended it.

None of her lectures made any difference; she loved him. She had no doubt that if Jason found her warm and soft and loving and in his bed he would not turn away. He would take what she offered and perhaps feel an obligation towards her. That was not enough. She loved him too much to try to trap him in a web of unwanted obligations.

'Separate bedrooms?' she echoed, adding a ripple of laughter. 'There's a door, a very usable door.'

'I watch old mystery movies on TV,' Emma snorted.

'Fine. So what do old movies have to do with the price of tea in China or anything else?' parried Katie, anxious to have this inquisition finished.

'If you take a length of thread and tie one end to the doorknob and tape the other end to the inside of the doorpost, can't nobody hardly see that thread, can't nobody open that door without breaking that thread. Three weeks and that thread ain't done nothing 'cept catch dust.'

'Mrs Parks!' Katie gasped.

Emma nodded and shook her finger at her. 'You get to pounding sand, girl, while you still got a rat to keep to home.'

The house was silent, the brood off to see the monsters and Jason checking the progress made on the renovation during the week. Katie tiptoed across her bedroom, cautiously sliding her eyes around the room, searching for any possible hiding place, in case Mrs Parks had sneaked back and hid. She rapped on the connecting door which had remained unlocked. There was nothing on this side Jason found even remotely interesting.

Much to her dismay, her rap was answered by footsteps and she found herself staring at Jason, bare-chested, wearing only Levis that slid over his flat stomach and muscled thighs as smoothly as a second skin. She tore her eyes from his tautly muscled body filling her with a renewed ache to truly be his woman.

She spied Emma's tattle-tale thread, a strip of Cellophane tape fluttering from its dangling end. 'Mrs

Parks,' she blurted, jerking the thread free from the doorknob and wadding it into a ball.

Her explanation was greeted by a moment of silence followed by a burst of laughter welling up out of his broad chest, throwing back his dark head to fill the room with the sound of his wholehearted delight. 'Nobody pulls the wool over Emma's eyes, not even her Baby Girl!'

His laughter died, faced by Katie's stricken look. 'She's not going to expose our little fraud, Kathleen,' he assured her, his fingers finding the curve of her neck.

'Do you have a neck thing or something?' Katie spluttered, knocking his caressing hand away. Chin up, eyes flaming with green fire, she struck with the last of her defences, the temper she had resolutely kept tucked in her back pocket since the day in the orchard.

'Neck thing?' asked Jason, goading her, encouraging her to argue with him, which would be an improvement over the busy silence she had been imposing.

'Yes! You know, some people have foot fetishes, is your thing necks? You're always hanging on my neck, like a vampire or something,' Katie said crossly.

'A neck thing?' Jason repeated slowly, his rejected fingers rubbing his strong chin thoughtfully. He certainly did, he wanted to start at her neck and work his way down, nibbling honey-gold skin all the way to her toes. 'I never thought about it before, but perhaps I do, Kathleen.'

'And you're always calling me Kathleen. Nobody calls me Kathleen,' she continued, the glint lurking in the azure depths of his eyes urging her on.

'It's your name, Kathleen.'

Katie glared, her mouth pulled into a firm line. He'd done it again. He didn't even argue fair. He argued with irrefutable facts.

She did the only thing she could do, she slammed the door in his face.

Supper and calling Jason to the house could only be delayed so long. Katie, acutely aware of just how alone they were and how close he was, responded to his attempts at dinner-table small talk with monosyllables and concentrated on eating. The one-sided conversation limped to a halt halfway through the main course.

Tossing his napkin on the table, Jason pushed his empty plate away. 'Káthleen, I do not bite,' he announced.

Katie slid her eyes in his direction. She studied the curve of his strong jaw, the firmness of his mouth. He didn't bite. He was much too civilised for that, unfortunately.

'No, you don't,' she agreed, and popped a bite of steak in her mouth, ending the conversation.

'I have been known to nibble on a neck now and then, though,' continued Jason, his low-pitched voice softening as he leaned close to Katie, his fingers finding and caressing the sensitive cord of her neck.

Inhaling the delicious reaction that began as a butterfly flutter and picked up intensity as it sped along her veins, Katie swallowed the chunk of meat and began choking in unromantic earnestness.

Realising she wasn't holding her throat playfully, Jason was beside her instantly, pulling her from the chair. He draped her over one arm and thumped her on the back, hard, between the shoulder blades. On the third blow the meat dislodged, popping out very much like a cork from a bottle. He poured her back in the chair he'd snatched her from, then wrapping his arms around her, he held her close.

'Feeling better?' he asked shakily, nuzzling to top of her head.

'Yes,' Katie managed to croak.

'Here, drink this.' He offered her a half-filled wine glass. Katie shook her head. At this moment she never wanted to eat or drink anything ever again.

Silent minutes ticked by, while Jason hovered over her chair.

'Feeling all right now?' His hands moved to caress her neck, discovering all sorts of sensitive little hollows and curves.

'Absolutely normal,' she assured him, regaining her voice. How normal she hoped he never found out. The weakness in her knees had nothing to do with almost choking, any more than her euphoric lightheadedness and the tingling warmth enveloping her could be blamed on a half a glass of wine she had consumed with supper. He was the intoxicant affecting her and he was a very potent vintage.

While she still had the will to resist, Katie planted her hands on the table and stood up.

'I'll just clear the table.'

'You don't have to do that right now,' coaxed Jason, his mouth finding the trail his fingers had blazed.

'I do!' Katie insisted, darting around the table and scooping up used dishes.

'I'll help you.'

'No!' Jerking her mouth into a smile, she snatched the plate he'd picked up and thrust Emma's wine at him. 'You sit! I mean—I mean, you're tired, Jason. You should sit down and relax and enjoy a leisurely after-dinner glass of wine,' she suggested, backing away.

'Not that tired,' Jason grated when she had scuttled from the room.

After adding their dishes to the load waiting in the dishwasher, Katie wasted as many minutes as she could making minute adjustments in their arrangement.

'Kathleen,' Jason announced from the doorway, 'the war is over.'

Her heart skipping crazily, Katie slammed the dishwasher shut and punched up the proper sequence on the control panel. Even his damn dishwasher was a computer.

'Yes,' she nodded, not having the slightest idea of what war he was talking about.

'The South surrendered.'

'Over a hundred years ago,' she added, mystified by his sudden interest in the Civil War.

'Missouri surrendered.'

'Missouri remained in the Union,' she corrected.

'Then why do I have the feeling that the Stauntons fought on the other side?' demanded Jason, advancing on her.

'Because they did.' Deserting the dishwasher, Katie backed along the counter, keeping her distance as he pursued her across the room. 'Well, some fought for the Union,' she admitted when she hit the angle of the counter's L. 'Made for interesting family reunions for a while,' she babbled desperately, inching towards the refrigerator.

'Without a doubt,' Jason grated. His mouth set in a grim line, he halted in the middle of the room, his feet firmly planted. 'Have you ever been drunk, Kathleen?'

Katie shook her head a quick, emphatic no. 'Once. It made me sick, very sick. Didn't like that,' she amended quickly, not adding that before being sick she'd been talkative, talkative and truthful, two things she didn't dare be at the present.

'I am going to get drunk—very drunk. Do you know what I do when I get drunk, Kathleen?' asked Jason, his eyes glittering with dangerous blue light.

Katie shook her head, her lips forming a silent no.

'Unless you want to find out, I strongly suggest that you stay away from the study tonight,' he warned, exchanging Mrs Parks' wine for the bottle of Bourbon in the kitchen cupboard.

Katie was still nodding her head when the study door slammed.

'Batter up!' Emma Parks shouted. She was in a foul

mood, sensing that her planned evening had gained nothing more than allowing her to brag that she'd been awake until the early hours of the morning.

Katie tapped the scrap of carpet that served as home plate for their two-base soft ball games with the tip of the bat. Catcher-umpire Parks had no more reason to be temperamental than she did. She'd spent their romantic evening in her bedroom reading a book that would have made more sense if she'd turned it upside down and read it backwards.

Katie took a practice swing and grinned a toothy snarl aimed at Jason pounding his fielder's mitt and calling time-honoured insults. If she was no batter, he was no fielder. She'd played ball in the side yard since before starting kindergarten. She knew exactly how hard to swing to send the ball arching skyward, falling just short of the first row of apple trees, barely in bounds and almost impossible to field. All she had to do was pretend the ball was his head.

The ball and bat connected with a solid thwack. Chance, screaming, 'I got it, I got it!' deserted pitcher's mound. Katie's confident lope turned into a flat-out run. Chance knew the vagaries of the side yard as well as she did and his pride was still stinging from her unfair slap at his driving skills.

Poppet, the next batter and youngest player, was guaranteed four strikes, unlimited balls, and could not be put out on a hit-and-run to first base. Poppet couldn't be put out, but Katie could and would be if she didn't make it to second base on her own hit. She rounded first base and saw the ball hit ground and bounce into Chance's waiting mitt. A grinning Jason crouched with one foot touching second base, waiting for the ball, waiting for her. Vowing that she would not be put out by him, Katie threw herself and slid, feet first, for second base.

It took some moments for her to realise that she

had stopped sliding very quickly and that one of the legs which should have been in front of her was under her. Quite dispassionately she thought of how many times she had told the little ones never to slide into base feet first because this could be the outcome. She observed the angle of her leg and considered the position of her foot, which was an impossible combination. Ankles didn't bend that way, not that far. She realised that, strangely, she was in no pain. In fact, she felt nothing other than amazement that Jason who should have tagged her was just standing there, staring at her.

'Are you all right?' he asked.

Katie looked straight into his eyes and wondered what kind of a fool could look at a woman with her leg twisted under her at an angle no self-respecting leg would ever attempt and calmly ask if she was all right.

'No,' she informed him airily. 'I think I broke something.'

Pride demanded that she brush aside his offer of aid and walk off the field unassisted. Unfortunately, her ankle declared itself a separate entity, free of pride, and rebelled when she tried to stand. She fell into Jason's arms, clutching at his strength. It hurt!

Jason sank to the ground, rocking her in his arms and crooning soothing nonsense. Soon other voices and hands joined him, patting her shyly and sobbing that she was going to be all right and angrily reminding her how many times she'd told them not to slide into base feet first.

Katie sniffed back a sob and attempted a brave smile while Jason kissed away the last tear and smoothed her hair away from her face. His eyes, infinitely sad and tender, searched her face. 'I'm sorry,' he whispered huskily.

Katie shook her head and touched the strong line of his jaw with her fingers. He had nothing to be sorry for;

she'd done it. Katie Clarie Staunton and her stubborn pride, they'd done it all by themselves.

Jason moved his head, guiding her fingers to his lips, and kissed them gently. Katie laid her head in the shelter of his shoulder. It was true, what every mother and child had known since the beginning of time, love could kiss away a hurt, even a one-sided love.

'Chance, get a board, this ankle is going to need support before we can move her. Emma, call the doctor and tell him we're on our way. Jeet, Poppet, dump all the ice you can find in a pillowcase and bring it to me. Bo, Rocky, get the back seat down and pile in some blankets and pillows for cushioning,' commanded Jason, bringing order out of chaos.

Katie burrowed deeper into the shelter of his arms. Pride would just have to wait its turn.

'It was bound to happen, sooner or later. I knew one of these days you boys would get tired of breaking your own arms and legs and start in on Katie,' Frank Carruthers, resembling an ageing football player more than a physician, boomed from the doorway of the packed examining room. 'And I think about half a dozen of you are going to have to retire to the waiting room.'

Five children instinctively crowded closer to Katie, determined to protect her from this new danger. They didn't care how many times he had stitched and plastered them back together, they had trusted doctors with their adults before and lost. They didn't intend to lose again.

'Is Katie going to die too?' Poppet wailed for all of them, wrapping both arms around Katie's arm.

Dr Carruthers' eyes flickered around the crowd of children, stiff with fear and ashen under their summer tans. 'No,' he vowed solemnly. 'But I need room to examine her and I'll need X-rays. As soon as I know anything I'll tell the nurse and she'll bring you all back. Okay? I'll let him stay,' he bargained, pointing to Jason.

'Come on, Poppet.' Chance scooped Poppet up and favoured the doctor with a slit-eyed glare to remind him that people who lied couldn't expect to live to a ripe old age.

After a swift cursory examination of her lesser wounds, Katie was X-rayed and given sufficient time to decide that Jason saw her lapse into clinging as nothing more than the after-shock of being hurt and frightened. He certainly showed no inclination to continue. He was as silent and remote as ever, giving the glass-fronted instrument cabinet his undivided attention.

Exhaling a shuddering breath, Katie folded her arms over her eyes. She hurt with an ache that went far beyond bones and muscles.

Jason's eyes flickered over the girl stretched out on the examining table. A man could do a lot of thinking in a few minutes. She wouldn't be here if he hadn't been there. Some things couldn't be caged.

Dr Carruthers burst into the room, flapping a pair of X-rays. 'You've got some kind of luck. It's not broken—why or how, I don't know, but it's not. It would be less painful if it——' He stopped mid-sentence and considered Jason carefully. 'You are this young woman's husband, aren't you? In the excitement I forgot to ask.'

Jason nodded, his dark brows gathering into impatient wings. 'Reese. Jason Reese.'

'Good luck.' A decidedly unprofessional glint invaded the doctor's eyes.

'I'm afraid you're going to have a disabled wife on your hands for a while,' he continued in a more professional manner. 'There's nothing much I can do right now except wrap it and send her home. You get the fun part, you get to keep her in bed. By that I mean rest, total bed rest. I don't want any more damage done to that ankle. I want her off her feet completely, and knowing Katie as well as I do, that's going to take some doing. Do it! Even if you have to sit on her, just don't bump the ankle.

'I don't believe there's been any permanent damage done. But just about everything that could be pulled has been, in directions they were never intended to go. All those muscles, tendons and ligaments need to be pampered and she'd going to be in a lot of pain tonight. That's why I'm going to give you a couple of pain pills. They're new and very potent. I think one would knock a horse out cold. Give her one, one only, when you get her home. The second, if she needs it, after midnight.

'Ice packs tonight, then moderate heat—a heating pad—for a couple of days. After tonight, any pain aspirin can't control, swelling, abnormal discolouration or fever, you get her back here immediately. Barring complications, I'll see you Tuesday afternoon, then we'll see if she needs a cast or if she can get by on crutches for a couple of weeks.'

The doctor snapped Katie's file closed. 'Any questions? Good, now let's get Attila and the Huns back in here before they decide to lynch me!'

It was a strange sensation but not unpleasant, Katie decided, to be detached from her body. Her mind was floating free and weightless while her encumbered body, growing heavier and more disorientated by the moment, sank. Dr Carruthers was right, those pills were something, and she was certainly feeling no pain.

She forced one of her ten-ton eyelids open and attempted to focus her eye. The door was open, someone or a pair of someones was peeping in. How many she could not be sure, it or they kept wandering, but then so did the door and the walls, for that matter.

Her hand jerked up and flopped back. 'Yi!' she greeted it/them. 'Yo figgle!'

When the apparition tittered Katie giggled too. A short circuit had developed between thought and speech, her brain would order a word but her mouth would deliver a garbled mish-mash, which didn't really make any difference since it was much too difficult to concentrate hard enough to remember what it was she had tried to say in the first place.

The apparition divided, disappeared, and became Jason standing over her. Katie grinned up at him. He had deserted his schematic drawings for her and all she had to do was sprain an ankle. It was worth it.

'You don't say?'

'Hup,' she agreed.

'Kathleen,' his strong bronzed fingers stroked her head, 'the doctor says you should be asleep by now.'

'Ho?' she mourned. The thought of disappointing Dr Carruthers or Jason brought tears to her eyes.

'What's wrong?'

Katie concentrated very hard. 'Runk?' she guessed.

'Close enough,' Jason chuckled softly. 'Now be a good little drunk, quit fighting it and pass out.'

'Shay,' she pleaded, clutching his hand.

'As long as you want me here,' he promised, kissing her eyelids closed.

Katie didn't want to wake up. She whimpered her protest against the pain prodding her to consciousness. 'Hurts,' she complained to the hand brushing her forehead.

'I know, I know,' crooned Jason. 'Swallow.'

She swallowed the pill without conscious thought, it was the water she wanted. She drank greedily and considered running her finger around the inside of the tumbler to collect the last few drops of precious moisture.

'Thirsty?' When she nodded, Jason carefully lifted her in his arms and surrounded her with a mound of pillows which had mysteriously appeared. 'Hot or cold?'

'Hot,' Katie decreed, even though she wanted something, anything cold. Her mind was becoming alert to the dangerous combination of his potent masculinity and her weakened condition. She needed distance and time to organise her resistance. 'There are orange and spice-flavoured tea-bags on the middle shelf of the left-hand cabinet by the sink.'

'Hungry?'

Katie considered ordering a complete meal which would keep him occupied in the kitchen until she passed out again. She shook her head; even more urgent than her need to keep distance between them was her desire for a drink.

She was already feeling the first giddy effects when Jason returned with a tray. Her request had been turned into a full-scale tea party, complete with a plate heaped with Emma's incredibly light baking powder biscuits, almost as delicious cold as they were hot from the oven.

'Numb yet?' he asked as he rearranged furniture for their feast.

Katie pinched her cheek. 'Almost.' She was much more interested in watching him. Even sitting in a rocking chair, pouring tea from a delicately fluted teapot, he was totally male, dominating the room and all in it by simply being there. 'You're going to make some lucky girl a terrific wife some day,' she joked, hoping to get her wandering mind back where it belonged.

'Think so?' His eyes and mouth softened with silent amusement as he handed her a cup of tea.

'Know so.' She ducked his infectious grin. She was walking a dangerous path, one that led nowhere. The pain of that knowledge tugged at her lips and lowered her eyes.

'Ankle still hurt?'

'Some,' she lied softly.

When she shook her head at the plate of biscuits he sighed, lifted her hand and filled it with half a biscuit lavishly spread with butter and strawberry jam. 'Eat— doctor's orders. Did your ever-so-great-grandmother actually have four husbands? I've wanted to ask you that ever since the first time I heard you tell that story. Poppet may prefer John Staunton's mama's hat, but I think I like Granny Anderson better.'

Katie smiled shyly. She hadn't realised that he listened in the evenings when the little ones gathered close and she spun out tale after tale. She liked the tale of the feisty old lady too, independent enough to outwit the United States government and live where she wanted and as she wanted. And what could be less dangerous than words limited to people who had lived a hundred and fifty years ago?

By the time Katie had relived the tale of Amanda Anderson, her three happily co-existent husbands and twelve strapping sons sending the sheriff scampering down the mountain understanding that folks' private lives was none of the law's concern she needed a second cup of tea. Telling how Eli Staunton had followed Mr Boone into Missouri when it was still Spanish Louisiana polished off the biscuits. Daniel Staunton was in the process of wandering off the trail from St Charles County to New Madrid County in search of earthquakes and ending up in Camden County when her tongue lost its agility and her mind began to play tricks.

'Walnut tree,' she murmured, her mind bursting with a luminescence as saddening as it was brilliant. When he bent near, she touched his hair, the colour of rich, hand-rubbed walnut. 'You're a walnut tree,' she explained.

'Why a walnut tree?' he asked as he completed his role as nursemaid and tucked her in bed.

'A walnut tree——' Katie paused, her underlip pushed out in concentration as she searched her foggy mind for words. 'A walnut tree self-pollinates.' She wagged her head woefully. 'Mr Walnut Tree doesn't need Mrs Walnut Tree, he's happy all by himself.'

'That makes us two of a kind, doesn't it?' His voice was the false hearty rasp reserved for inquisitive children who had said something they shouldn't have said or a man hiding behind words.

'No,' mourned Katie, her words and thoughts slurring. Her hand jerked out to him and flopped back to her breast. 'Holly berry.'

'Why a holly berry?'

She sighed heavily. Poor walnut tree, he really didn't know. She held up two fingers. 'Takes two. Mrs Holly Berry has to have Mr Holly Berry or there's no little Holly Berries.' An errant tear rolled down her cheek. Walnut trees couldn't help being walnut trees any more than holly berries could help being holly berries. 'Dumb ol' holly berry,' she murmured, 'had to go and fall in love with a walnut tree.'

Katie mended quickly. The foggy dreams of midnight tea-parties and walnut trees standing guard over her sleep, reviewed in the sharp light of day, were relegated to their rightful place—figments of a fevered imagination.

Reluctantly her heart listened to her head. A real tea-party would have left evidence, there was none. There was no tray of dishes, the rocking chair was where it belonged, the small walnut table she had dreamed he had set their feast on was spotless and in its proper corner. No crumbs, no extra pillows, because it had never happened. Even more damning, when she gave in to her last hope and asked, Jason admitted hearing her cry and giving her the second dream-inducing pill. He made no allusion to a midnight kitchen raid or any story-telling session. There was no evidence, because it hadn't happened. Walnut trees didn't walk or talk and Jason Reese hadn't been part of a mad tea-party.

Aged July gave way to drowsy August. Katie threw

herself into enjoying the summer and the company of the brood. She had her boys and her Poppet and her hills. Who in their right mind would ask for more? And if she found Jason's eyes silently questioning her, it was only natural impatience. She was an expensive investment and showing no return.

CHAPTER EIGHT

KATIE watched the small plane taxi to a halt and disgorge its passengers. The gnawing fear that had been growing since Jason's abrupt command to prepare for guests spread from her churning stomach to the tips of her fingers. Two corporate officers plus one wife for the weekend carried the distinct aroma of a test.

Mentally she dusted her hands of any doubts about her abilities. She had aided in entertaining the parade of people Tommie Staunton had insisted on dragging home, ranging from chicken thieves to United States senators. Nothing Jason Reese could produce would top the characters Magistrate T. A. Staunton had passed sentence on and then invited to stay for supper. Nothing could be wilier than the smiling men hoping to influence State Senator Staunton, also invited home to be wined, dined, charmed and have their brains picked.

Katie was the mistress of the fine art of smiling and saying nothing, of keeping her ears open and her mouth shut. Grandma Staunton had always said that Katie could charm a bird out of a tree if she put her mind to it. Rapt attention, a soft smile, simple bedazzlement by their superior talents and achievements, it worked every time, and Jason's birds wouldn't be any different.

And if she kept telling herself that long enough she might begin to believe it. Pasting on her most effective smile, Katie added a stern reminder that it wasn't necessary for her to believe, only that they believe. Jason had paid for a hospitality centre, she was going to deliver one, the best one there ever had been. If she could not have his love, she would earn his respect. Besides, entertaining would put more people between them and busy her mind with thoughts other than Jason.

Slipping out of the driver's seat of the truck, Katie smiled shyly at the handsome, dark-haired woman marching towards her. Her heart lurched against her ribs as she fought down the urge to run and hide. The woman resembled a Sherman tank, not in size, in intent. Her target was Katie and anything or anybody foolish enough to get in her path would be run down.

'Mrs Catalano?' ventured Katie, hoping she was wrong and by some miracle this charging female was pursuing something other than her.

Viewed at close range the woman was even more formidable. Sleek, fortyish and fashionable, of above average height and trim figured, her dark eyes raked Katie with haughty distaste, taking in and rejecting every detail of her dress and person. Her mouth was a bitter red slash curled with contempt.

'Yes.' The mouth smiled, a fleeting grimace quickly recalled.

'I'm Kathleen Staunton Reese,' Katie announced, chin angling, her hands remaining at her side. She offered her hand only to friends, and this was no friend.

Again the red mouth twisted into a false smile. 'It's easy to see why Jay suddenly found the Ozarks so intriguing!'

Ignoring the acid hiss that turned what should have been a compliment into an insult, Katie waved the woman to the truck. 'Please get in, Mrs Catalano, and we'll save the men a walk.'

Seated in the passenger's seat, the woman flicked imaginary dust from her skirt. 'How did you meet Jay?'

'Poppet—Alicia—goes to school with my boys. She stayed with us——'

'Ah, yes, the baby-sitter. Onwards and upwards to bigger and better things,' the woman sneered, her narrowed eyes once more travelling suggestively over Katie's body.

Katie's temper soared. To hell with a tradition of hospitality! To hell with manners. For a nickel she'd scratch out the woman's eyeballs! Folding her arms over the steering wheel, she smiled a toothy warning at the smug female next to her. 'Are you naturally hateful, Mrs Catalano, or do you work at it?'

'Oh, I work at it, honey, I work at it,' the woman purred.

'It shows,' Katie assured her as she thrust the key into the ignition and slammed the truck into gear.

The atmosphere in the truck crackled with tension. Katie kept her eyes resolutely focused ahead. Forty-eight hours trapped in close proximity with this snarling hellcat, her claws already bared, her fangs dripping venom, promised to be nothing short of a slow journey through perdition. More frustrating, she had arrived prepared to slash and backstab. Katie was certain of that, as sure as she was that the woman was an expert. She was prepared for curiosity, avid curiosity; an unknown, unseen, sudden wife was bound to pique minds. But overt malice, that she had not expected.

The men piled a variety of luggage in the rear cargo space that made Katie wonder, uncomfortably, if they were moving in for good.

'You two reprobates climb in the back,' Jason ordered cheerfully, claiming the driver's seat as his own.

Katie saw a glimmer of excitement lurking in the azure depths of his eyes as he tilted her face up and kissed her lightly. She brushed the firm line of his jaw with her lips and clung to him for a precious moment before settling into the shelter of his shoulder. Even if it was only a game on his part, she needed something strong and protective right now.

His eyes questioned her, she had redoubled her efforts to avoid him since her attack of fantasy tea-parties, to the point of almost throwing children into the space separating them. Business, her arched eyebrow informed him.

'I'm forgetting my manners. Kathleen Staunton Reese, and I have to remember the Staunton or she forgets the Reese,' Jason announced in a teasing aside that made Katie wonder what he was up to. 'This is Rab Catalano, our resident wizard,' he twisted and jerked his head at the slight, balding little man behind him.

'Mr Catalano.' Katie unleashed her most devastating smile. His eyes behind their wire rim spectacles glittered with curiosity but lacked any hint of his wife's open hostility.

'And Tom Bennett, our favourite whizz kid.' Jason indicated the second man, young, blond and terribly earnest, who acknowledged her with a brisk nod.

'Are you related to T. A. Staunton?' asked Tom Bennett, leaning forward, urging her to answer yes and quickly.

'My father,' Katie admitted.

'Thought so.' He grinned a smile that could have lit up half the county. 'Conservation had a good friend in the Senator.'

Katie's lashes fluttered down to hide her eyes. She hadn't expected a stranger to know her father. His life had been snuffed out when only his constituents and ardent conservationsists knew him and his ideals.

'You've done your homework, Tom,' grated Jason, his arm closing possessively around Katie's shoulder.

'If you hadn't been so close-mouthed, Jay, I would have put two and two together a lot sooner. But then you couldn't have kept me away,' Bennett answered eagerly, ignoring the chilly edge on his friend's voice.

Katie relaxed, the firm warmth of Jason's body pressed to hers. It was going to be all right. She had met Tom Bennett a hundred times before, in earnest young men arguing earnest arguments. Rab Catalano wanted to be won over. That left only the heller on her right. She peeped at the woman, who was silently gnawing on the corner of her lip, to keep the venom from spilling over in public, no doubt. Oh well, Katie decided, two out of three wasn't bad and she would smile and play dumb until her teeth ached. She'd done it before.

She frowned as another problem wormed its way back into her conscious thoughts. Jason would have to be warned about the new shift in beds. But there were other problems to be faced first, getting the brood through mannersome introductions, supper, a long evening of smiling in the face of that woman's devious insults.

'Oh, my God!' the woman at Katie's side gasped when Jason turned into the lane exposing the house, dominating the hollow with its quiet, rugged beauty. 'That house must be at least a hundred years old and in perfect condition. How did you ever find it, Jay?'

Jason chuckled and kissed Katie. 'It was easy, June— I married the owner.'

The woman swallowed a hasty, 'Oh,' and remained silent until the truck stopped in front of the house. Climbing out, she stared at the line-up of waiting children. Her mouth opened and closed silently as her eyes bounced from Poppet to Chance, counting heads along the way.

'My, my my,' she babbled, grabbing Poppet and turning her round and round like a top. 'Haven't you grown, Alicia?'

'Yup,' Poppet giggled. 'But you have to call me Poppet now, Aunt June. That's my name, Alicia Marie Poppet Staunton Reese, just like Katie.' Jeeter nudged her in the ribs and frowned at the ground. 'Oh! I'm Alicia Marie Reese, Mr and Mrs Catalano, Mr Bennet. I'm pleased to meet you.'

'Oh my!' June Catalano warbled. 'Such a formal

young lady! Do you suppose this grown-up person has one kiss left for her poor old Auntie June?'

Poppet giggled and complied, planting solemn little kisses all around. Katie's heart dropped to the level of her toenails. She was feuding with a woman known, either by blood or courtesy, as Auntie June. It was going to be a very long weekend.

'Come and meet the rest of our family,' invited Jason with a certain pride, indicating the silent boys.

'Jeeter.'

'John Carter Staunton, ma'am.' Jeeter bobbed his head and stared at his shoes, inching backwards, away from this unknown, untried stranger.

'Bo.'

'Robert Lee Staunton.' Bo jammed his hands into his pockets to keep his feet from wandering, but he clearly wanted to be anywhere but where he was.

'Rocky.'

'Randall Lee Jackson,' Rocky blurted in a single breath. Since Bo wasn't moving neither did he.

'And Chance.'

'Charles Allen Staunton.' Tight-lipped, Chance nodded curtly and held his ground. He also wished to be elsewhere.

And if Katie wasn't mistaken, so did June Catalano. The woman was pale and her smile becoming even more strained as her eyes darted from boy to boy. With her eyes Katie motioned the brood to the truck and the luggage they were to deliver to the proper rooms before they politely disappeared.

'Ask Mrs Parks to hold supper, I want to show Rab and Tom around a bit,' Jason whispered.

Katie nodded absently, so preoccupied she was almost unaware of Jason's hands circling her waist and his breath teasing her ear. The boys' discomfort was no mystery. They were instinctively shy. If given their heads, they would bolt for the hills at the first sign of an outsider. June Catalano wasn't mountain bred and certainly not shy.

'Would you like to freshen up, Mrs Catalano?' she asked in her best gracious-hostess tones.

'I need a drink,' the other woman commanded.

'Lemonade? Coffee?'

'Scotch, straight up, a double.'

'Of course,' murmured Katie, ushering her into the house.

The woman tossed the offered drink down her throat with a practised twist of her wrist. Drawing a deep breath, she straightened her jacket and smoothed her skirt. 'Those are not your children,' she accused.

'They're my younger brothers.'

'Your brothers,' June Catalano repeated. 'Certainly. How simple! How silly of me to not have realised that. Brothers.' She drew another deep breath and plunged forward. 'Have you lived in this charming old house long?'

'All my life.'

'All your life.' June Catalano paled to an even more unhealthy shade of ash-grey and sank into a chair. 'Your father was a Senator?' There was a note of desperation in her voice begging Katie to say it wasn't so.

'Just a state Senator,' Katie soothed. The woman was possibly an alcoholic, maybe crazy, definitely not well. 'Mrs Catalano, are you ill?'

The woman stared into Katie's concern-clouded eyes. 'Yes,' she shook her head emphatically, 'terribly ill. I'm suffering from terminal stupidity complicated by acute embarrassment.' Crawling out of the chair, she leaned over and patted her upthrust rear. 'Kick it, I deserve it.'

Katie stared, dumbfounded. She had met many unusual people in her short lifetime, but never anyone quite like June Catalano. Northerners, she knew, were strange people, but she was certain this one was strange even for them.

'Would you like another drink?' she suggested doubtfully.

'I'd like that,' June Catalano agreed firmly, straightening up. Smiling tightly, she handed Katie her drained glass. 'But first I'm going to change your marital status to widow.'

Katie jerked her face into a smile. She was certain she'd heard correctly. 'I'd be terribly upset if you did that, Mrs Catalano,' she protested pleasantly, shoving the refilled glass at the woman.

'Oh, I'm only going to half kill him, honey, and let the other half suffer,' June Catalano promised grimly. 'He did this on purpose, you know.'

'Oh?' Katie tilted her head and smiled her encouragement to the other woman to keep talking. Jason had outdone her father; he'd handed her a certifiable lunatic.

'Yes. I'll get him for this, just see if I don't!' June Catalano vowed, pacing the room in quick, jerky little steps. She stopped and pressed well manicured fingers to her forehead. 'Oh God! You must think I'm crazy—totally bonkers. Not that I blame you. That is the most reasonable explanation, isn't it?' She aimed a toothy leer at Katie. 'I don't suppose you'd like to listen to a good explanation?'

Katie was definitely interested in hearing any explanation; good, bad or indifferent. Hospitality and manners, however, did not allow for the open questioning of a guest or her actions.

'Travelling is very unsettling,' she assured the other woman.

'She's tactful too,' June Catalano informed the ceiling. 'I insist. And if you'll trade this for the coffee you offered first, about a gallon of it, because I'm going to need that much to wash down the amount of crow I'm going to eat, I'll tell you the whole story.'

That was an offer Katie couldn't resist, and since

the woman was insisting it was only good manners to listen.

June Catalano sipped her coffee and murmured an appreciative, 'Very good,' before setting the delicate cup down with a firm clink.

'Intelligent men are notoriously stupid about women,' she stated matter-of-factly, borrowing her ex-professor husband's technique of beginning a lecture or a conversation with a statement outrageous enough to catch and hold attention. 'They are,' she challenged before Katie could object. 'Jay had been smarter than most, I will admit that. But the second week end in a row that I had Rab all to myself, no Jay, no computers, I knew something was up. Three in a row and I knew it had to be a woman.

'Asking Rab was useless—if it's not a computer he doesn't notice. Jay simply was not talking, only disappearing and looking very pleased about it. Then he just up and announced that he'd got married. Period! Well?' June paused to throw her hands in the air. 'I did the only thing I could do—I put my ear to the grapevine and listened. And believe me, when it's the boss who's being mysterious the grapevine buzzes. Especially if he's young, good looking and available.

'I found out that you had Alicia, and you wouldn't have been the first one to realise that Jay's weak spot is Alicia and tried that angle. I discovered there were several other children, who I rashly assumed were your sons. I heard the ridiculous rumour that you'd actually worked in a bar.' Her dark eyes, glittering with curiosity, fastened on Katie.

'I did,' Katie assured her, her chin angling. 'And my grandfather did transport moonshine during the depression.'

'My dad ran a gambling room in the garage. Well, it was either that or selling apples,' June Catalano confided with a wry grimace.

Sobering, she pushed her mouth into a stern line. 'All of which is no excuse for my actions. I came here determined to put you in your place and I find that you are in your place. It's lovely, as you are.'

Her curiosity far from satisfied, Katie sensed that that was the extent of June Catalano's confession for the time being. She was being offered what amounted to a cease-fire. She took it.

'Are you interested in antiques, Mrs Catalano?' she asked, offering a safe topic that could be exploited for hours, days.

'Love them,' June Catalano vowed.

There was enough time before dinner for Katie to show the downstairs. June Catalano possessed a solid knowledge that convinced Katie her professed addiction to antiques was genuine. Not that she would have rejected the other woman's truce if she had thought it false. Their conversation, limited by tacit agreement to the nineteenth century, was pleasant if highly forgetable.

It was a surprisingly pleasant evening, with the men reappearing to lend a masculine tone to the conversation over one of Emma's superb offerings, before excusing themselves and disappearing into the study with their plans and drawings. June was content with finishing her tour of the house and grounds and a history lesson. Sipping coffee and relaxing in wicker chairs, they watched from the dancing floor as the little ones chased fireflies in the gathering dusk and listened to the crickets fiddle their orchestrated warning that summer was waning and autumn near.

Katie rested her head against the back of her chair and closed her eyes for a moment. It was going better than she had dared hope. If June Catalano wasn't exactly bubbling with good fellowship at least she was no longer snarling and her reasoning and actions were no longer completely mystifying.

June enjoyed verbal brawling. She shocked her opponent into silence and then went for the jugular. A very effective technique, as Katie had already learned. She was relieved and amused to learn that she wasn't the sole victim. Tom Bennett had been slashed to shreds before he could unfold his napkin and had conceded defeat before he picked up his fork. June and Jason had exchanged friendly thrusts throughout the meal, neither a clear victor, both enjoying the battle. Rab Catalano, whom Katie had misjudged as a quiet little mouse of a man, returned his wife's jabs with practised ease, often besting her—a turn of events which June seemed to relish. Katie, a grateful non-combatant, had listened and enjoyed the lively debates which weren't that different from the politicking she'd been raised on.

Opening her eyes, she slid a covert glance in June's direction. As dramatic and domineering as she was, and she was definitely both, Katie found herself liking the woman.

'Have you known Jason long?' asked Katie. She was prying, or preparing to, and not being at all delicate about it. Delicacy would only have drawn one of June's barbed retorts.

'Only since the year one,' drawled June, keeping her eyes on the playing children. 'Are you trying to pump me?'

'Yes,' Katie admitted.

'Good. Because I planned to do the same thing to you, as soon as I got you softened up.' June chuckled softly and turned her full attention on Katie. 'Now that the preliminaries are out of the way, who goes first? I suppose I should, I owe you one.

'How long have I known Jay? Since he breezed into one of Rab's classes and talked him into trading a professorship with tenure for twenty-five per cent of a dream. For which I will be eternally grateful. Of course there were times when I thought I might end up scrubbing floors. It was touch and go. But obviously we prospered and now I can be as obnoxious as I please. Even to the boss's wife,' June added, aiming a smug but non-threatening smile at Katie.

'It sounds easy now, but it wasn't. Even though Rab is one of the best computer men in the country, the world, it took Jay to tie it all up in a nice neat package and sell it. He's done a little of everything. He even worked on the assembly line. I've even known him to go out on a maintenance call. Who better? He designed them, built them, sold them, who better to repair them, he'd say.' She paused, enjoying the memories of the struggles the fledgling company had overcome. 'Of course he doesn't have to any more, hasn't for some time. Jay could just sit back and relax, but he won't. He's no more capable of doing that than Rab is. Today's state of the art is tomorrow's antique, or if they guess wrong, yesterday's. They like that, though, they're in love with the damn things. Ann and I——' June looked away, momentarily silent.

'The subject will come up eventually,' she challenged. 'You know who Ann is, was?'

'Jason's wife,' Katie murmured. Her hands involuntarily tightened, her nails dug into her palms. Part of her wanted to know more, part of her wanted to run away and hide.

'Jay's first wife. If I can remember that, you can,' June prompted kindly. 'And of course you're curious about her—you're only human. She was a beautiful girl, inside as well as outside, and Jay loved her. That's not what you wanted to hear, but it's the truth. When she died it was as if part of him died too. This summer when I saw Jay coming alive I was so afraid for him. Men aren't the unfeeling, uncaring bastards we like to pretend they are. They can be hurt too. Too many people, men as well as women, but women especially see a wealthy man and never get past the wealth to the man. He's been through hell once, I didn't want him hurt again.'

She reached for Katie's hand and squeezed it. Her brash façade melted exposing genuine concern. 'What I'm trying to say is, I was afraid, but now I'm glad for him and I wish you both every happiness in the world for a very long time to come.' Leaning closer, she hugged Katie quickly, her lips brushing her cheek.

Scanning the darkening hills, June settled into her chair. Her lapse into sentimentality was over, she was once more the grande dame in control.

'Jay made the same mistake, didn't he?' she announced, her dark eyes glittering obsidian-bright, daring Katie to contradict her.

'The boys?' asked Katie, realising that having made a mistake June Catalano wouldn't let it rest easily. 'Yes, he did.'

'Well, that explains it, doesn't it?'

'Yes,' Katie agreed. 'It' didn't explain anything to her, but apparently it did to June, for which she would be eternally grateful and not ask any questions. The tissue of lies she was living wouldn't bear many of June's sharp probes, and she didn't want the ghost of Ann, the wife Jason had loved and lost, to come any closer.

The conversation wandered through several harmless topics, always circling back to politics. Katie offered several carefully edited anecdotes which seemed to prove to June's satisfaction that she did know 'those' people. She countered with stories and famous names of her own. Thankfully, Katie slipped into her natural role of listener.

Dusk became full dark.

'Bedtime!' called Katie, opening her arms to Poppet galloping towards her on Chance's shoulders.

'Can't we wait for Daddy?' pleaded Poppet the first of her delaying actions as she snuggled in Katie's arms.

'Knowing your father, Rab and Tom, they may stay locked up in there until noon tomorrow. Those three!' June snorted.

'Those three what?' Jason grinned at them from the porch, his eyes dancing with mischief.

'I was about to warn Kathleen that the day will come when she'll wish there was another woman. Flesh and blood she can fight, but micro-chips are impossible to beat—I know, I've been trying for years. And you're the worst of the bunch, Jay.'

'Not true,' denied Jason, taking Poppet from Katie. 'Impossible for an ordinary flesh and blood woman perhaps, but Kathleen is no ordinary woman. She's a witch, didn't she tell you?' He gently pinched Poppet's nose. 'She put a spell on me and she's going to put one on you right now.'

Leading the way to Poppet's bed, Katie wished she was a witch, then she could conjure a spell or brew a love potion. But she wasn't a witch, and the only spell she knew was a bit of loving fakery to close eyes, not open them.

'I'll move Poppet in with me when I go to bed. Mr and Mrs Catalano are in her room and Mr Bennett is in the spare room. Someone had to double up,' Katie explained in the hallway after the bedtime ritual of kisses and eye-gluing was over and Poppet safely tucked in her father's bed.

When Jason nodded his understanding and approval of her sound logic, Katie realised that June was right, there was no fighting the computers which had cast their bewitching spell over him.

'You haven't lost your flair for quiet bombshells, Jay,' June chided when they reappeared. 'To tell me your wife is a witch and then walk out—that was intended to keep me on the edge of my seat!'

Chuckling softly, Jason led Katie to her wicker chair and perched on the broad sweep of its arm. His hand sought and found the sensitive nape of her neck. 'I should have warned you about June. She's crazy about witches, ghosties and things that go bump in the night.'

'Parapsychology is a legitimate branch of scientific research,' insisted June, drawing herself up in her chair, preparing for an enjoyable verbal skirmish.

Comfortably out of the conversational limelight, Katie relaxed and allowed the ebb and flow of friendly debate to wash around her. It was a lively and varied conversation bouncing from serious to frivolous, punctuated with throaty chuckles and sharp exclamations. A friendly star winked and Katie winked back. If she could have a wish she would wish this night never to end. That it would always remain a clear summer night with the hills standing guard and Jason holding her close.

She wasn't aware of Jason abandoning the arm of her chair for the chair itself, nor did she know when she began sharing his drink. She only knew it was right, so very right, to lay her head on his chest and listen to the low rumble of his voice and the strong steady beat of his heart. That it was soothing and exciting to experience the casual exploration of his stroking hands.

Only when June shook her head at a second hearty yawn did Katie remember her manners and show her guest to bed.

Her mind still wrapped in Jason's arms, Katie prepared for bed. Shaking her hair free of its coil, she slipped into a simple shift dress trimmed with a froth of ivory lace. She wandered about the room, her mind unwilling to surrender the magic of the night. She ran her fingers over the carved finial of a bedpost, the Louisiana Bride's marriage bed. Once she had believed that the incised diamond pattern of the pineapple, as pine-cones were then called, a frontier symbol of hospitality, was magic, a good luck charm, and that if she rubbed it just right her wish would come true. If only, if only—she shook her head; 'if only' did not exist.

She moved Poppet into her bed and willed her mind to cease its restless turning. The bewitching evening had been a well-acted day dream, no more real than magic pineapple/pine-cones or midnight tea-parties with walnut trees. Reality was an alarm clock and a house full of guests.

The floorboards creaked their welcome to the whispering men in the hallway. Two doors opened and closed. The house slept.

Katie jerked bolt upright, clutching the sheet to her chin. The house had either sprouted a ghost or someone was trying to get into her room. She fell back against the pillow with a relieved sigh. It was only Jason standing in the doorway. Of course, the others would have thought it strange, to say the least, to see him go to bed in his child's room. Jason being the logical man he always was had picked up the loose ends her schemes invariably left lying around and had tied them into neat bows. He was using the connecting door, that was all.

'Goodnight,' she whispered, secretly apologising for the jumble of frantic and sensuous thoughts that had raced through her heated brain.

'Congratulations. You made three brilliant conquests today.' Jason smiled his intriguing lopsided grin and freed his shirt tails from his trousers. 'You handled June just right. But I knew you would. After all, you remembered to say excuse me and please when you knew you had two brothers in the living room fighting over which one got to shoot the stranger on the porch. Remember?'

A blush lowered Katie's lashes. Being told that she'd handled June Catalano at all was a compliment, but she'd always hoped that he hadn't heard Bo and Rocky that first day. She peeped at him through the fringe of her lashes, not knowing quite what to say.

'What are you doing?' she gasped. It was perfectly obvious what he was doing. He was undressing.

'Going to bed.'

'This is my bed!' She raised her sheet barrier.

'I know.'

'Poppet's here,' she warned, inching across the bed, putting a fraction of the necessary distance between his potent masculinity and her stirring senses.

'I'll move her back to her own bed, where she belongs.'

'You'll wake her.'

'No.' Shaking his head, Jason scooped his sleeping daughter into his arms. 'We both know that this one could sleep through the end of the world. She didn't wake up when you moved her in here; she won't wake up when I move her back. And this way you won't have to explain how she got from one bed to another.'

'Jason Reese, you get yourself out of here—right now!' Katie ordered in a whisper when he returned minus Poppet.

'No, Kathleen. I'm sleeping here, in this bed, with you.'

He meant it. Katie's heart lurched crazily against her ribs. He meant exactly what he said. He was either crazy drunk or just plain crazy, because only a fool named Jason Reese would think they could sleep together in the same bed and not——

'I'll sleep in there,' she babbled, pointing to the connecting door.

'No, Kathleen. You're sleeping here.' Jason sat on the edge of the bed and continued his leisurely disrobing.

'Jason—now, Jason,' Katie pleaded, scrambling out the other side, seeking relief from the turmoil he created in her. 'Sometimes when a man is tired and has had a bit to drink, he doesn't quite think straight. I suggest that we discuss this in the morning, when we're both clear-headed.'

'No.' Shaking his head, Jason followed her desperate backwards flight across the room, stalking her with the lithe grace and intensity of a hungry panther.

'I'll scream,' she threatened, near tears. That was a wall behind her. She couldn't run any further. If he came any closer she would be lost, stripped of all her defences. One touch and she would no longer care that it was only a fool's game gone out of control.

'Kathleen,' he reached out, pulling her to him, his fingers caressing her skull, tangling in the silken mass of her hair, 'do you want me to leave?'

Dropping her head, Katie held back the shameful truth. She wanted him to stay, to never leave her, to love her, to make love to her now and always. That she craved him, her body ached with wanting him.

Capturing her lowered chin, Jason forced her eyes to meet his. 'I want you, I want to make love to you,' he whispered huskily. 'I've wanted you since the first time I saw you standing in the sunlight, skin the colour of wild honey. I knew then that if I bit you, you'd taste of honey, wild and sweet and something no man had ever sampled before.'

She stared up at him, her soft lips parted but mute and trembling with the wonder of his words. Questions, doubts, fears, hopes going beyond words raised her hands to test the truth of the strong lines of his face. The firm, warm reality of him surged through her fingertips, unleashing a flood of longing that left her weak and breathless in its wake.

He rasped her name, his lips exploring her face, brushing her eyelids, her mouth, the curve of her jaw. His teeth nipped her earlobe, his quickening breath fanning the growing flames of desire searing her senses. Strong, sure fingers sought and found the ribbon tie of her gown to push aside the confining fabric, freeing it to fall in a pool of lace and cotton at her feet. Freeing them to discover what they had so long denied.

His arms tightened, crushing her tautening breasts to his rock-hard chest, heightening her already explosive yearnings. Descending, his hands caressed and teased their way to her hips, lingering, coaxing, until she surrendered completely.

She clung to him, head thrown back, eyes closed, savouring the shudders of pleasure exploding along every nerve. A low moan was torn from her lips as she felt the pulsing hardness of his manhood. Answering her cry, Jason lifted her in his arms and carried her to their marriage bed.

Katie stirred, stretching with languid pleasure against his length. Kissing his hand flung possessively over her, she sat up. The sense of sated contentment that had enveloped her lingered, half closing her eyes and curving her lips into a sensuous smile. 'My man,' she murmured, her fingers brushing the thick walnut-brown hair from his forehead.

She had no wish to wake Jason, even the sun was still abed. She wanted only to look at him, to ponder the wonder of him. Sleep softened the deep lines of his face. His lashes curved against his cheeks in sleep made his somehow vulnerable. She brushed her lips across his mouth and allowed her fingers to stroke his whisker-shadowed face.

His eyes flickered open, their crystal depths clouded with sleep. 'What are you doing?' he murmured, stroking her hair, lazily pulling her to him.

'Looking at you.' Her lashes fluttered down to meet her warming cheeks.

'Is that all you want to do, look?' Jason teased gently, crooking his thumb under her lowered chin.

Katie shook her head, her smile no longer shy. 'No,' she whispered huskily. 'Not nearly all.'

Resting her head on his sweat-dampened chest, she listened to the thunder of his heart. Sleepily content but feeling more alive than she had ever felt before, she purred happily, rolling her shoulders and arching her back to greet his stroking hand. Lacking the urgency of before, they had made love slowly, revelling in the discovery of each other.

'You know,' she wondered aloud drowsily, giving voice to an errant thought flitting through her mind, 'I could have put Jeeter in with Chance and Poppet in his room. Then——'

'Then I would have gone out and found another guest and another and another until you had guests hanging out the windows and no bed but mine to crawl into.' Jason chuckled indulgently, his eyes lazily challenging her to question his motives or actions.

'You planned this,' Katie accused, too pleased to be angry.

'Um-hum.' He grinned and kissed her eyelids. 'I'm a patient man, Kathleen, but even I have my limits. You were driving me crazy. I couldn't work, I couldn't think. But nothing I did touched you.'

He grabbed her shoulders and rolled on top of her, pinning her to the bed. 'I don't keep fishing poles in the kitchen, Mr Reese. I pay my own bills, Mr Reese. Your gifts are not welcome, Mr Reese. Yes, sir and no, sir, and kindly go jump in the lake, sir. I want to marry you, sir, but only temporarily, Mr Reese, sir,' he growled with mock severity.

'Oh God,' he vowed, collapsing on her, crushing her to him. 'You drove me crazy! All I could do was watch you touching them, loving them, and all the time I wanted to shake you and tell you, love me too, Katie. And you couldn't even stand to be in the same room alone with me.' He silenced her attempted denial with a kiss. 'Oh, you had me fooled, Kathleen Reese, until you swallowed Dr Carruthers' truth serum. Then I found out all about walnut trees and holly berry trees and mountain wives.'

Katie smiled, relishing the sweet taste of his words, storing them away for later wonder. Wrinkling her nose, she pushed against his superior weight. 'If you knew so much, what took you so long, Mr Reese?' she demanded as she aimed a loving blow at his side.

'What took me so long?' he howled, rolling off her. 'Woman, trying to get you alone, by yourself, with no kids. I love them all, Kathleen, but you couldn't have stayed closer to them if you'd all been Siamese sextuplets.' He folded her in his arms and nuzzled her cheek. 'That's what took me so long, and I'm so glad we're finally here.'

She hushed him with a kiss, her heart singing with a joy too full for mere words. She wanted to share with him what she could not find words to say.

Slipping out of bed, she held out her hand to him. 'Come with me.'

She raised her face to taste the morning and greet her hills. The morning haze hung heavy and low, shrouding the hollow in silent enchantment, muting even the birds.

They became a part of the silence, walking carefully and quietly. They forded the creek at the shallows above the swimming hole. Choosing the gentler eastern slope, Katie picked her way along the hidden path to the place her heart had come to claim as its own.

They were no longer on original Staunton land. In 1882 John Staunton had bought himself a mountain, or part of one. He had paid cash-money for it too, much to the head-scratching wonderment of his neighbours. Because that was one of the times when the normal hard times had got downright mean. And this land was so vertical any livestock grazed on it had to have one pair of short legs and one pair of long ones or they'd fall right off the hillside.

If his contemporaries hadn't been able to understand his desire for a bit of land too poor to raise much more than rocks, his great-great-granddaughter could. John

Staunton had bought the mountain to feed his soul. It was to this place she came to ease her hurts, share her joys, or simply find the space and quiet for thought. Since she had brought the thought of Jason Reese to the mountain often, it was only right to bring the man.

From here they could see across to other hills or down to the hollow below slumbering under its billowing blanket of ground fog. They listened to the silence that was not silent but alive and vibrant with the stirrings of the mountain readying for a new day.

She introduced him to some of her wild kin, creatures of the mountain, rightfully wary but not adverse to sharing their hillside with one who came so often and quietly, never molesting, never questioning the right of the mouse to the acorn or the hawk to the mouse.

A squirrel, defying the laws of gravity, hung upside down from a nearby tree trunk. His expressive tail curved in a twitching question mark. Was she or wasn't she going to offer a treat? Katie flicked her hand, miming his talkative tail, and chattered at him in excellent imitation squirrel scolding before reaching into her shirt pocket for the cookie she had hidden there. The squirrel scampered up the tree, crouching on his hind legs in the main crotch, and waited for her to deposit her offering at the foot of his tree and retreat a proper respectful distance.

The squirrel halted mid-trunk, his tail jerking to alert attention. 'This is Jason, we mean you no harm,' Katie assured him. The squirrel waltzed sideways around the tree trunk as greed battled with caution. Greed won. He scrambled head-first for the cookie, grabbed it running and scampered back up, body and magnificent tail flattened against the tree.

As he sat in his lofty perch, his tail jerked with spasmodic laughter. Squirrel had outwitted human again. He had the treat and she had nothing, not so much as a single hair from his tail.

Shaking with silent laughter, Katie curled in Jason's arms. She had a special love for God's own clowns. She never tired of their graceful acrobatics or their sheer joy in living.

'You belong here,' Jason murmured, his arms tightening as his lips brushed her hair. 'You'd die in a cage.'

'I belong here,' she corrected, twisting in his arms to wrap her arms around his neck and kiss him.

CHAPTER NINE

KATIE rapped softly on the closed study door. Jason had signalled midnight before shutting himself away. It was now five after. She interpreted the 'Um-m-m,' from the other side as meaning, 'Come in.'

Men! A smile tugged at her mouth as she enjoyed a moment of feminine superiority. They were nothing more than little boys grown tall. Give them a new toy and they had no sense, none at all. That was what his computers were, overgrown toys, and he delighted in playing with them.

He glanced up, his mouth curving into a lopsided apology. 'I, ah——' Katie nodded her understanding. He had lost track of time, he often did. 'Almost done,' he promised.

Katie nodded again, resisting the urge to brush the walnut-brown hair away from his forehead and claim his attention. She set the coffee tray on a side table and curled up in a chair. The coffee was in a thermal jug, and after five weekends of being a real wife, she simply enjoyed watching him.

His eyes traced the pattern of a diagram, pleased as lines and symbols wended their logical way across the paper. Logic—Katie cupped her chin in her hand, her eyes softening as she watched her man lose himself in the beguiling maze. She had been reading everything she could get her hands on about computers and the computer revolution. While it and they lacked the fascination to her that they held for Jason, she could understand it better. Jason had a mind as restless as a mountain man's feet. He liked to explore new frontiers in his head and then build them into something real.

And each new computer frontier conquered spawned half a dozen new and more exciting wildernesses. Her competition was micro-chips and modules, as illogical as that sounded.

Reaching out, she folded the schematic drawing over his hand. Enough. If left to himself Jason would trace and calculate until dawn and then start over.

'June was right,' she whispered, bringing her mouth to within inches of his. 'You're in love with those things.'

'What things?' he laughed, pulling her to his lap. 'You're the only thing I see.' His eyes clouded, searching her face. 'Kathleen, are you happy with the way things are?'

She kissed him hard and buried her head in his shoulder. She couldn't very well tell him the truth. She was jealous of his machines. She hated the way things were. Five long, lonely days and nights with him so far away in exchange for two so sweet and soon gone. He loved his machines: building them, explaining them, selling them. He was addicted to them. They came along with him on paper to the weekend retreat he didn't want to share with anyone else. There were times when the truth was better left unsaid. If he was happy, she was happy.

'Yes,' she lied, 'very happy.'

Jason's arms surrounding her tightened, crushing her to him. The pictures and realtor's description of the Victorian house he had found and pictured her in would stay in his briefcase. Easing his bruising hold, he tasted the warm honey-gold of her skin until the bitter loneliness of the week was gone.

'What would you like from San Francisco?' he asked, his plan for a delayed honeymoon put aside with the photographs of the house.

'San Francisco?' Katie repeated, fear growing and twisting in her stomach, overpowering the sweet ache of his touch.

'Industry show. The industry show of the year opens Wednesday for an eight-day run,' Jason explained more bluntly then he'd planned.

Eight days, Katie's heart cried, Wednesday to Wednesday. The machines were gobbling the little bit of him she had.

'You,' she admitted frankly, adding a careless shrug to show she wasn't serious. 'You pick. Surprise me— I've always thought one of the best parts of a gift was wondering what it is.'

'I have to be there. People want to see the man, and I'm the man.'

'I know.' Katie stopped his explanation with a kiss. It was only one weekend out of a lifetime of weekends. 'Just don't forget you're not one of your machines. You do need to eat and sleep,' she lectured, adding an impish grin that didn't quite reach her eyes.

'Actually the work is so well mixed with play it can hardly be called work, unless you count eating and drinking and swapping tales. Plenty of time for sightseeing. You haven't seen fog until you've seen it come rolling in off the ocean. Then there's the Golden Gate Bridge and Fisherman's Wharf, the bay, cable cars. Hills. There are hills in San Francisco too, you know,' Jason added to his list of sights he hoped might entice her from her hills to be with him.

'You do have a thing for hills, don't you?' Katie teased, biting back the impulse to invite herself along. 'I know something else you have a bit of a thing for,' she whispered huskily, pillowing his head in the warm swell of her breasts. She'd love him so hard, so completely, Sunday night would never come and he would never leave her.

Sunday night came and took Jason away. The lonely week and lonelier weekend came and went too. As the count down of days neared its end, Katie pushed aside the gnawing fear that this Friday might come and not bring Jason with it.

Thursday dawned with the crisp blue and pure gold promise of a perfect autumn day. School claimed the brood and Emma Parks went off to town and the grocery store with a monumental shopping list anticipating Jason's homecoming. The perfect day tempted Katie to abandon the house for the autumn brilliance of the hills. She resisted the urge to ramble by polishing polished surfaces and dusting dustfree corners. She hoped Jason would call and tell her he missed her so much he was deserting his machines a day early and coming home.

The telephone remained obstinately silent. Leaving the back door open so she could hear, Katie wandered outside. The hills called, softly, sleepily, asking if she was as well prepared as they were for winter, the time of cold and snow coming soon. A woolly bear caterpillar, his black-banded brown body undulating with his many-footed gait, inched across the sun warmed stones of the dancing floor. Katie knelt and watched. The weather forecasting bands were wide, warning of heavy snow. All the creatures seemed to know, pelts were thick and the gatherers busy storing their caches. How did they know such things?

The telephone's shrill demand for attention jerked Katie from her reverie and sent her sprinting for the house. A little breathless, she answered on the third ring.

'Kathleen, this is June,' June Catalano announced brusquely when Katie answered. 'You might as well know from the very beginning, I'm calling to give you holy hell.'

'What have I done now?' laughed Katie, recovering from her disappointment that it wasn't Jason and preparing for one of June's harangues.

'Well, you got sick, that's what you did. Don't you

know that's practically illegal?' When Katie, too stunned to think of an answer, said nothing, June's brash scolding mellowed to concern. 'Now you know I was just trying to give you a hard time, honey. I really called to see if you're feeling better.'

'Yes, I'm feeling much better,' Katie assured her, not sure how much better she was supposed to feel since she hadn't known she'd been sick.

'That's good. Jay said it was just a 'flu bug. We missed you, so be warned, next show I will personally drag you along, hospital bed and all, if necessary!'

'I hope such drastic measures won't be necessary,' Katie parried, feeling that somehow she'd come in on the middle of this conversation and not sure that she wanted to hear the rest.

'Oh, and how are all the little kiddies?'

'Fine,' Katie answered honestly, still a little bewildered.

'Well, that's a small miracle, isn't it? Jay said that's what you were worried about mostly, that they'd catch it from you and you didn't want to leave your Mrs Parks with that threat hanging over her head.'

'Yes. Very lucky, not so much as a sniffle,' Katie answered, pushing the words past the lump thickening in her throat. Jason had lied.

'I'll say,' June insisted, launching into a dramatic recital of her woes the winter her two children had decided to have measles, mumps and chickenpox all in a row, effectively imprisoning her for more than two months.

Filling the pauses in June's flow of words with what she hoped were the right responses, Katie sagged against the wall, her jaw clenched to keep back the tears. Jason had lied. She had been expected in San Francisco, and he had explained her absence by claiming illness. He was so ashamed of his hillbilly of a wife he had lied rather than take her with him.

Jason had lied.

Angling her chin and staring at the wall opposite, Katie refused to cry. She still had her pride. When June laughingly repeated Jason's claim that he couldn't move Katie to Chicago until he found a house with a yard big enough to hold a mountain, Katie laughed too. Somehow she held on to her pride until June hung up.

Her breath coming in tearing sobs, Katie fled to her hills. The house was too small and she didn't want to be anywhere near a telephone.

As she walked, hurt became anger, first directed at June Catalano. 'Don't you ever call me again!' Katie hissed, swiping at tears with the back of her hand as she struggled blindly uphill, admitting even as she railed at the absent woman that June had done nothing except verify what she'd feared and refused to see.

Blind—she'd been blind and stupid, a dumb hillbilly. Because she hadn't needed to say, 'I love you', she had blindly assumed Jason felt the same. She'd been a fool dreaming a fool's dream, but she was awake now and looking reality square in the face. His wife? Hardly, she was his court jester, something he kept around for amusement, something to laugh at with her cut-off blue jeans and sing-song accent, and his whore, ready and willing whenever he decided to drop by. She was a fine joke, and as long as no one saw her he would keep her tucked away in her hills dreaming her foolish dreams.

He was a liar, and she was a fool.

Finding the oak tree she had come to so often and brought Jason to, Katie huddled on the ground at its base hugging her misery to her. All the nagging little doubts and questions she had pushed away and ignored came bubbling to the surface. When they talked it was of little unimportant things. Never the past, never the future, nothing of his present.

Now that nagging little voice in her mind would not be stilled. Why, it demanded, did Jason exclude her so completely, not just from the past where Ann, the wife he had loved and lost, lived, but from all his life, his todays and tomorrows as well? Because he was so ashamed of her, that was why. Because he never intended that she be a part of his life. What other reason could there be?

Her arms squeezing her legs tightly to enclose the ache in her heart, Katie rested her forehead on her knees. She was a fool, ten times a fool. Jason had never said he loved her, only that he wanted to make love to her and she had been too blind and deaf and dumb to know the difference.

'No more,' she vowed, raising her face to the listening hills, her chin angling proudly.

To be nothing would be better than being his fool, and that was all she had ever been her wounded pride screamed at her aching heart. She would make no accusation, demand no explanation, neither would she give any. She would let him wonder, let his mind wander down dark corridors of sleepless nights, not knowing, never knowing why. Their agreement, their contract had never been modified. Jason had simply availed himself of the full hospitality of the house, hospitality she had eagerly offered. She would simply end it, as was her right.

'So be it,' she whispered to the hills.

Emma had returned during Katie's absence. She was putting away groceries and humming tunelessly to herself when the screen door squeaked its welcome to Katie.

'Where you been, girl?' she demanded. 'No need to answer that—I know.' She sounded her deep bullfrog snort and shook her head in fond exasperation at Katie's rambling. 'Mr Jay had to call twice, 'cause there was no answer the first time. He's coming home.'

'Fine,' Katie answered bitterly. The sooner he came the sooner it would be done.

'Fine?' Emma Parks snorted, for the first time turning to really look at Katie. 'You coming down with something? You look like something the cat brought in! Get yourself over here,' she ordered as she descended on Katie.

'No fever,' she wondered aloud, patting Katie's forehead and cheeks with the back of her hand. 'Fact is, you're chilled,' she fussed.

'I think I'm coming down with the 'flu,' announced Katie, freeing herself of Emma's unwanted attention. 'In fact, I'm sure of it. I heard it was going around. I think I'll just go upstairs and lie down for a while.'

'You just do that, honey,' Emma agreed, nodding and frowning her disbelief at Katie's back.

Forced into bed by her own assertion, Katie could do nothing but stay there and tolerate Mrs Parks' tender if sceptical ministrations and refine her plans for vengeance. Freed from school and warned by Emma, the brood tiptoed past Katie's door. Occasionally, every five minutes or so, one or more would peep in to see if she was feeling better. It wasn't difficult for Katie to convince the trusting children that she was too ill to pick up Jason but that they should all go as usual. If Mrs Parks had any doubts she kept them to herself.

Once they were gone Katie worked quickly, stripping the house and her life of Jason Reese. Her mouth curved into a bitter smile as she observed the fruits of her labour, one medium-sized cardboard box with room left over. He had never intended to make his stay permanent.

She toted the box to the study and tossed in his calculator and portable dictating machine before folding the cover flaps in place. It would furnish the dash of irony needed, she decided, to offer him a drink and then call an end to what she had proposed in this very room.

She showered and changed into rust-brown slacks

and co-ordinated top shimmering with all the colours of
the hills in autumn only to exchange them for a dress of
cool jade green. She wanted to present an image as cold
and hard as the semi-precious stone. He had done the
unforgivable, and pride demanded vengeance. Silent
vengeance, pride whispered.

They were back; Katie went to meet them. Nervously
smoothing her skirt over her hips, she ordered her
quivering stomach and legs to not disgrace her.

Jason kissed her tenderly, his hands capturing and
caressing her upturned face. The thought that his ego-
saving white lie had somehow bounced back and
infected her with his concocted 'flu clouded his face.
'You are pale! Come on, back to bed before you infect
the whole crew.'

She resolutely quashed the hopeful leap of her heart.
Of course he was concerned. He saw only the naïve
mountain girl he had left behind a million years ago,
content with the crumbs of his life. It was on the tip of
her tongue to tell him that broken dreams weren't
contagious.

'I have something to tell you first, in the study,' she
announced in a husky whisper as she freed herself of his
embrace.

She concentrated on putting ice cubes in squat,
heavy-bottomed glasses and holding the neck of the
decanter against the rim of the glass. Her hands were
shaking so much there was no other way to steady
them. Her chin jerked up to steady the thunder of her
heart as she handed him his drink and backed away. He
looked so pleased and eager to hear.

Her foot touched the solid, inanimate wall of the box
containing his clothes. Tossing her head back, she
rasied her glass in salute and kicked the box forward
and watched it slide a crazy sideways course across the
carpet to his feet.

'I want you out of my house, tonight. Now.'

'What?'

Her wounded pride exulted. He had the look of a poleaxed ox, stunned.

'I'm terminating our contract as of now. Your services are no longer required, Mr Reese.' Her mouth curved into an icy smile. Creating pain did not heal a hurt, but it was a balm of sorts. Now he shared the bitter taste of betrayal.

'Damn you!' Jason hurled his drink. Glass and ice shattered against the smoke-stained stones of the fireplace. Whisky and soot dripped on to the ashes of a dead fire. The only sound in the room was the rasp of his breathing.

'Services!' Jason echoed. His first thought when she had said she had something to tell him was that her 'flu was a little morning sickness.

'Stud services?' he grated. The first time she had poured a drink for him in this room she had said she wanted a baby for this house and that a newspaper ad was as good a way as any to get it.

He shook his head slowly, his face chilling with fury as he descended on her. She wasn't serious, she couldn't be. His hands tangled in her hair, forcing her head back. 'No.'

The air crackled with the tension of two strong wills colliding. Katie pulled free of his hold, which quickly lost much of its power. She backed away, shivering with the emotions battling within her. Her fingers fumbled for the brass-covered finger-hold in the sliding door behind her.

'Goodbye, Mr Reese.' She forced her mouth into something resembling a disdainful sneer and disappeared through the sliver of space she had opened in the wall.

Vengeance gained, Katie fled to her bedroom, to hide behind doors she could lock. Numb and empty, she stared out the window, not seeing the hills or hearing the wind mourning for her.

She heard a door slam and heavy male steps. It was Jason, his long legs carrying him to the truck, taking strong, sure steps that left no time for looking back. She squeezed her eyes shut, holding back useless tears. She had told him to go, he was going.

'You could have said something,' she whispered. 'All you would have had to say was, I love you. I would have believed you.'

The pulse of the house slowed. The little ones straggled to bed, stopping to hope Katie was feeling better and to repeat Emma's tale of an emergency calling Jason away. Emma came too, offering food.

Katie shook her head. 'Tomorrow. I'll eat tomorrow,' she promised. Tomorrow she would eat and talk and laugh, get on with living. Tomorrow or some tomorrow, but not tonight. There was no living in her tonight, only emptiness.

'But you need to eat tonight,' persisted Emma. 'Mr Jay said to not be waiting on him. He might not even get back tonight.'

Or any night, Katie thought. The emptiness of the lifetime ahead clawed at her. 'I won't starve before morning,' she said.

'A cup of sweet tea might settle your stomach.' Emma cocked a hopeful eyebrow. Tea was one of her two sovereign remedies.

'No.' Tea. Tea-parties and walnut trees. Jason. It was one thing to banish Jason from her house, quite another to remove him from her heart.

'Hot toddy?' Emma offered her second and most powerful cure-all.

Again Katie refused, kissing the old woman's leathery cheek. 'And don't be climbing those steps again tonight. If I change my mind I'll do my own fetching and carrying.'

'You'll do no such thing,' Emma protested. 'I'm

sleeping upstairs tonight. I'll be right across the hall. You need me, you give a yell.'

'I will,' Katie promised, with no intention of doing so.

Katie waited for Emma to shuffle across to her own room, then she shut and locked her door. There had never been a locked door in the house that she could remember, now there were two. She went to bed, but only to doze fitfully, waking at every whisper of sound which was never Jason. He was never coming back.

She woke with every nerve tingling. Vehicles, like people, each have their own unique set of sounds. After driving the truck for four years she knew its every squeak and rattle. She raced to the window, her heart, not knowing if it should leap or stop, did a little of both. Dizzy with joy and relief, Katie rested her forehead against the cool pane of the window. Jason was back.

Pulling the corners of her mouth down and forcing her eyes to look away, she reviled herself for such foolishness. He had most likely just remembered that he had no clothes. Well, he could just get his clothes and be on his way—not that she cared one bit about what he did.

She tossed her head, chin angling with defiant pride. That had better be all he planned to do, not that there was much more he could do. There were only two doors leading into this room, both solid oak, both locked up tight, and she had the only key. Mr Jason Reese was just going to have to go peddle his wares elsewhere—not that she gave a tinker's damn what he did.

She tiptoed back to bed, listening carefully. What was taking him so long? What was he doing down there, prowling around in the dark? What she really should do was go down there and tell him that he wasn't taking that truck anywhere. Fine thing! Him just hopping in and taking off, leaving them clear out here with no way to get anywhere. It would have been a fine mess if one of the little ones had broken a leg or got bitten by a snake.

Katie was in the midst of fabricating a marvellous fantasy with the entire brood succumbing to broken bones and raging fevers when she heard a step creak. She jerked up in bed, her heart crashing against her ribs, and her eyes scanned the shadowy dark. She heard it again.

That Jason Reese, her mind spluttered, comes sneaking home and doesn't even have the good sense to sneak! Not that it was going to do him one bit of good. She snapped on the small bedside lamp and aimed a haughty sneer at the locked door. There was nothing he could do.

As she watched the doorknob in the hallway door quietly, slowly turned, then turned back. Footsteps moved away, down the hall. He could have at least rattled it or given the door a shove with his shoulder, to make sure it wasn't stuck, or so it seemed to her.

There was a soft rap on the connecting door and a whispered order, 'Kathleen, open this door!'

Chin angling, Katie folded her arms under her breasts and stared at the far wall. She'd open that door when hell froze over.

'Kathleen, open this door!'

Katie smiled a Cheshire Cat grin and shook her head. He was beginning to sound a wee bit perturbed.

'Kathleen, I'm a patient man, but if you don't open this door in ten seconds, I will!'

Katie hooked her finger through the shoelace loop tied to the big brass key and twirled it. That was one inch of solid, well seasoned oak, locked up tight, and she had the only key.

'Not likely!' she sang loud enough for him to hear.

'You won't open this door?' asked Jason, enunciating each word carefully, clearly.

'No, Mr Jason Almighty Dollar Reese, I will not.'

She heard the preliminary thud and felt the wall shudder and settle back. She grinned at the ceiling and laid back to enjoy the show. He could stay out there all night and beat himself bloody. It wasn't going to do him one bit of good. None!

A resounding crack jolted her eyes open. The door groaned and tilted to a drunken angle, its hinges screwed into thin air. As she watched a pair of strong male hands grasped the hinged side and pulled the door free of the lock.

'You broke my door!' she gasped, scrunching down, hiding under the sheet.

'I ought to break your damned neck,' Jason growled.

Katie gaped at him, her eyes wide, her lips forming a worried O. He wasn't just angry, he was furious. He meant it.

'Get dressed.'

She refused. Her head jerked with quick little spasms of denial as she inched across the bed.

'You won't get dressed?' He glared down at her, his eyes glittering dangerously, his broad chest heaving.

Katie shook her head again, this time managing a firm, 'No!' Her chin angled, assuming its fighting stance. Folding her arms, she addressed the wall, 'I'm not getting dressed and you can't make me.'

'Suit yourself,' warned Jason.

Katie glimpsed his move to capture her out of the corner of her eye and dived for the floor, only to find her ankles caught in an iron grip. Twisting, intending to hit whatever she could, she found herself fighting with the sheet which was tangling her arms and restricting her movements. Hissing her frustration, she pushed and pulled to no avail. The sheet was a living thing, wrapping itself around her tighter and tighter.

'Damn you, Jason Reese!' she spat. It wasn't the sheet, it was him. He was sitting on her, pulling the sheet around her shoulders, forcing her arms to her sides, passing the ends under her and back, ending with two corners tied in a neat double knot over her waist.

She kicked, not at him, as he was out of reach, but at the bed to gain leverage, to throw him off balance and roll away. He sighed, the heavy sigh of a man deeply aggrieved, and slid off and completed his packaging, knotting the last two corners over her ankles.

After adjusting a wrinkle here and there, he nodded, pleased with his handiwork. She was trussed up tighter than a caterpillar in a cocoon.

'I'll kill you!' Katie vowed, glaring daggers at him. 'You turn me loose right now, Jason Reese, or I'll give you what for!'

'No.' He rejected her threat with a firm shake of his head. He'd spent half the night driving and walking in circles, trying to figure out what went on inside that head of hers. Now he was going to find out. 'For once in your life, Kathleen Reese, you are going to stay right here and talk to me.'

'I'll scream,' she threatened.

Jason held his hands out, palms up, inviting her to carry out her threat.

Growling, she arched her back and strained against her bonds. 'I hate you!' she snarled, powerless to do anything else.

'Then allow me to scream for you,' offered Jason, picking her up and roaring for Mrs Parks.

'Yes, sir. Yes, Mr Jay.' Emma stood in the broken doorway, surrounded by five goggle-eyed children, bobbing her head and trying not to stare.

'Mrs Reese and I are going out,' announced Jason.

'Yes, sir,' Emma agreed, as if broken doors and sheet-wrapped wives were every day occurrences.

'I'm not sure when we'll be back.'

'Yes, sir. Ain't nothing here I can't handle,' Emma encouraged.

'All right, everybody back to bed,' ordered Jason, sending four of them scurrying away.

Chance lingered, his mouth pursed, his fingers studying the jagged holes the screws had left in the doorpost. Hope lifted Katie's heart. Chance wasn't full grown yet, but he was topping six foot and had the wiry strength of a farm boy who thought nothing of tossing hay bales around all day.

Chance frowned and jammed his hands into his pockets. 'Want me to fix that while you're gone?'

'No,' Jason rumbled thoughtfully. 'It would be a shame to have to go through all this again next week.'

'Got a point there,' Chance agreed, nodding, avoiding his sister's eyes, not hearing her pained groan.

'Mr Jay.' Emma fluttered her hands at him, stopping his march down the hall with his captive. 'If I remember rightly, there's a law still on the books that says a man can beat his wife if he don't use a stick no bigger round than his thumb.'

'Thank you, Emma. I'll keep that in mind,' said Jason, continuing his leisurely stroll.

Katie twisted her head until she could see Mrs Parks over his shoulder. 'Thanks,' she mouthed. 'Thanks a lot!'

Emma smiled beatifically and waggled her fingers. 'Now you have yourself a good time, Miss Katie, and don't you worry none about nothing round here.'

Jason propped Katie on the passenger's side of the front seat. She closed her eyes and turned her head. He didn't have to enjoy her total humiliation quite so much.

He pulled her resisting body to him. 'Kathleen, you're going to have to lean on me or you'll fall over.'

'I'd rather fall,' she told him, turning her head away.

'I know you would, but I won't let you,' he surrounded her with his arm and drew her into the strength of his body.

'I don't want you!' Katie hissed, the angle of her chin denying the want in her eyes.

'I want you,' he whispered, his lips brushing hers, caressing her neck.

Katie struggled to free herself before his lies could catch and wound her again. 'This is called kidnapping, Jason Reese. You'd best turn me loose and get yourself gone before I get the law on you!'

'No,' he denied her order with quiet firmness.

She glared at him, so calm, so sure of himself. 'I hate you!' she spat.

'I love you.' Capturing her chin, Jason turned her to him and kissed her tenderly.

'I can still bite,' she warned, shaking her head in a half-hearted attempt to free herself of his touch.

'Kathleen,' Jason sighed, 'I'm not a mind-reader. Don't you think it's time you told me what's going on?'

'Told you what? I've already had my say,' she huffed. 'You'd best get on with your kidnapping, Mr Reese, before they decide you're having car trouble and come out to help.' Her attempt at flippancy was betrayed by a sob in her throat. There was no fight left in her, only hurt and confusion.

'Don't do that,' Jason commanded softly, capturing her chin and forcing her averted eyes to meet his. 'Don't turn away and shut me out.'

'I'm not the one doing the shutting out,' Katie insisted, jerking free before he could see and enjoy the tears welling in her eyes.

Wrapping her in his arms, Jason held her close until her struggles to rid herself of him ceased.

'Kathleen, I don't like waking up in the morning and not finding you beside me, any more than I like coming home at night to nothing. But I can't commute eight hundred miles a day or run my business from a farmhouse kitchen. I don't know what else to do.'

'I'll bet you don't. I'll just bet you don't!' Katie

snapped. Looking past him, ignoring the tears spilling down her cheeks, she realised he never had, never would consider the alternative, taking her with him. 'Well, I won't be your weekend wife. I won't be something existing on the fringes of your life, something you're so ashamed of you won't be seen with it. You go back to your ghosts and your machines. You love them, then you go make love to them. You leave me be!'

'Ann,' Jason exhaled, his shoulders lumping in defeat.

'My name's Katie. Don't you ever make that mistake again!' Katie hissed.

'That was no mistake. I know who you are,' Jason grated, catching her face between his hands. 'Yes, I loved her. I'm just like you, Kathleen, I won't apologise for the past. I won't apologise for Ann. I loved her. She was my first love. Not even for you would I pretend those years with her didn't happen, because they did, and they were good years. But they're gone. Neither those years nor she have anything to do with the way I feel about you. I love you and I don't want to lose you.'

'Except that there's no room for me. She has the past and your machines have the future, and that leaves nothing for me.'

'That's not true and you know it!'

'Do I?' Katie challenged. 'You bought a baby-sitting service with a few interesting fringe benefits thrown in. I know, I'm the one who proposed it. A purely business proposition, remember?'

'No,' Jason denied firmly, realising how lacerated that stiff-necked, stubborn pride of hers was. 'I married a very stubborn woman who told me if I didn't she'd ask the next man who came down the road. And you'd have done it too, if for no other reason than to show me that you could. I couldn't risk that, I couldn't risk losing you. Even though that wasn't the way I wanted it, I didn't care. I would have taken you any way I could have got you, because I wanted you. Not for business, not for my daughter, for me. I'm greedy, I want you in my life.'

'Then why don't you take me with you?' Katie cried.

'How?' he asked, tracing the shining trail of tears down her cheek with the tips of his fingers. 'How do I lock up the sun or put something as free as the wind in a cage? How do I take you to a place where the hills are all brick and steel and the valleys are concrete? Where trees grow in pots and the morning mist is mostly exhaust fumes? How do I tame my proud lady, gentle her to my touch, and not break her spirit?'

'By saying, come with me,' Katie whispered. 'Jason, you're my mountains and my sky. I don't need any other if I have you.'

Untying his neat knots, Jason freed her. Catching her face in his hands, he held her away, his eyes searching her face, leaving her no place to hide or any desire to do so.

'Then come with me. Be with me, because I need you. I've been out in the cold for so long, Kathleen. I need you—I need your warmth and your love. I want you. I want you beside me sharing the joys and the worries too. I want to have children with you. I want to grow old with you, because I love you and my life would be so empty without you.'

'Oh, Jason, no emptier than mine would be without you.' The words were torn from her with a shuddering sob that drew her to him, wrapping her arms around his neck and burying her head in his shoulder.

Tenderly he raised her tear-washed face to his, offering a kiss that needed no words to explain it.

Share the joys and sorrows
of real-life love with
Harlequin American Romance!™

GET THIS BOOK
FREE as your introduction to
Harlequin American Romance —
an exciting series of romance
novels written especially for
the American woman of today.

Mail to:
Harlequin Reader Service

In the U.S.
2504 West Southern Ave.
Tempe, AZ 85282

In Canada
P.O. Box 2800, Postal Station A
5170 Yonge St., Willowdale, Ont. M2N 6J3

YES! I want to be one of the first to discover
Harlequin American Romance. Send me FREE and without
obligation *Twice in a Lifetime*. If you do not hear from me after I
have examined my FREE book, please send me the 4 new
Harlequin American Romances each month as soon as they
come off the presses. I understand that I will be billed only $2.25
for each book (total $9.00). There are no shipping or handling
charges. There is no minimum number of books that I have to
purchase. In fact, I may cancel this arrangement at any time.
Twice in a Lifetime is mine to keep as a FREE gift, even if I do not
buy any additional books.   **154 BPA NAZE**

Name	(please print)

Address	Apt. no.

City	State/Prov.	Zip/Postal Code

Signature (If under 18, parent or guardian must sign.)

This offer is limited to one order per household and not valid to current Harlequin
American Romance subscribers. We reserve the right to exercise discretion in
granting membership. If price changes are necessary, you will be notified.
Offer expires September 30, 1985

AMR-SUB-1